ONE SHADE OF GRAY

NEW YORK TIMES BEST-SELLING AUTHOR
MONICA CORWIN

ONE SHADE OF GRAY

Copyright © 2017 by Monica Corwin

All rights reserved. No part of this book may be reproduced in any form or by any electronic or mechanical means, including information storage and retrieval systems, without written permission from the author, except for the use of brief quotations in a book review.

Cover design by Covers by Christian

Book design by Inkstain Design Studio

Editing by Evident Ink

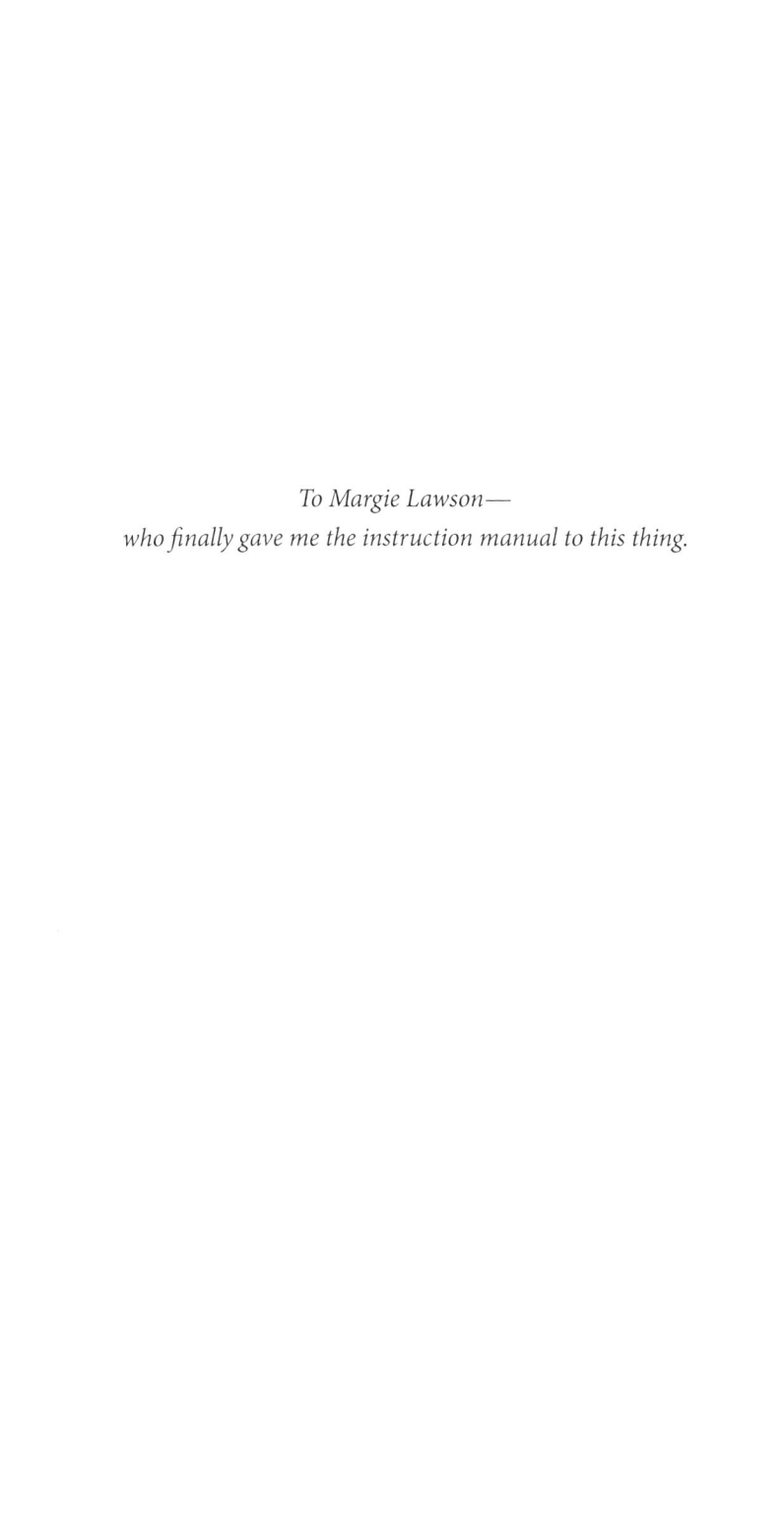

To Margie Lawson—
who finally gave me the instruction manual to this thing.

AUTHOR'S NOTE

My Dearest Readers,

Dorian Gray has been one of my favorite characters since I was a teenager. Like King Arthur, he was one of my first book boyfriends, ok more like my book bad boy. This book is a love note to him and a book I fell in love with. Any mistakes made here are my own and not reflective of The Picture of Dorian Gray. Furthermore, I hope no one takes my use of Dorian and his source as offensive. I only commandeered him a short while and I promise I will put him back where I found him.

XOXO

Monica

One Shade of Gray

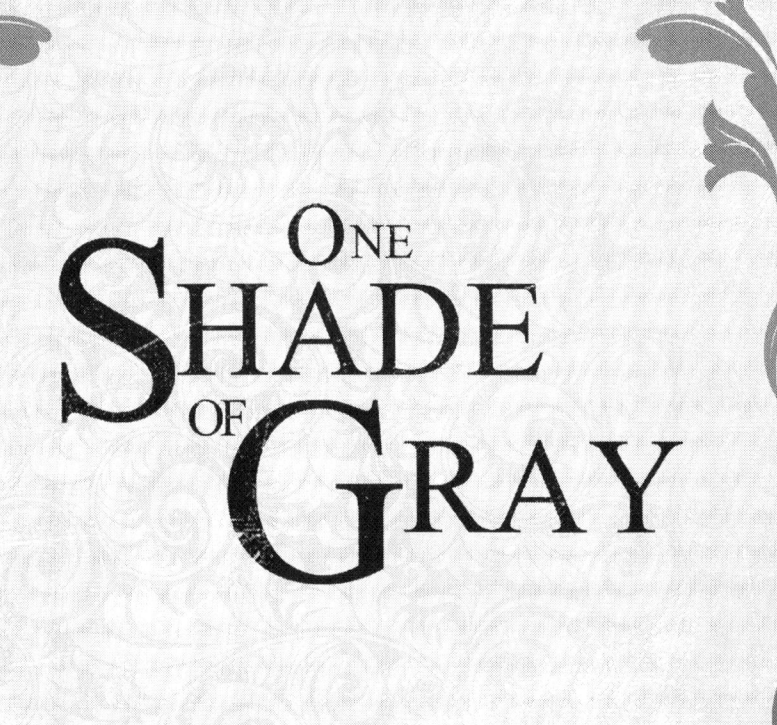

IZZY

A GIRL KNOWS WHEN SHE IS being followed. Just because the man was more or less my boss—my insufferably arrogant and oh so hot boss—didn't mean I should allow it. In fact, I considered myself quite solicitous in reigning in my urge to knee him in the balls.

I jerked to a halt in the middle of the *Rue Des Barres* and spun to confront him, but he must have stopped before I did. He now stood near a café, looking quite at home in his couture black Sandro suit, despite the casual tourist crowd oohing and ahhing over fresh croissant.

Any other day I might have ignored his presence and continued to the theater, but today I had been pushed to my limit. He was always watching me, and he'd no doubt witnessed me dump an entire espresso down the front of my cream blouse. So instead of heading straight to work, I drew myself up, made sure my red lipstick was smooth and my pixie cut ruffled just the right way before taking practiced steps across the cobblestones toward him. I could break an ankle on some of them, even in flats.

He stayed and surveyed my progress, making me doubt he had been the one trekking behind me since I left my apartment, until the innocence on his face caused a sense of foolishness to descend as I finally reached him. I skipped the pleasantries. "Why are you following me?"

His perfectly arched eyebrows rose a millimeter and I had to resist the urge to lick my thumb and muss them up. I also needed to get the name of his stylist.

A few weighted seconds passed and then the look of intense study on his face cleared to one of suave charm. It was so smooth I wondered if he kept masks in his back pocket to rotate. Or maybe he had practice at concealing his emotions. Or maybe he didn't have emotions.

He answered before my brain went too far off the rails. "I think perhaps we were going in the same direction."

No. I shook my head with all the dignity I could muster against that knee-bender of a smile. "You've been following me for two months. Ever since I took over the production of *Romeo and Juliet*. I know who you are Mr. Gray, I'm not an idiot."

His smile silkily shifted into something else, that caused the hairs on my arms to stand on end. "*Mon Coeur*, I very much doubt you know me at all."

Standing face to face with him was very different than seeing him hovering at the back of the theater, or passing him on a staircase. He wasn't much taller than my five-foot eight but his presence seemed larger somehow. His golden hair and deep blue eyes spoke of a man much older than the mid-twenties I thought him to be.

His voice broke my study of him now. "You did consider that we work in the same location?"

It sounded like a question but also a statement. One of those billionaire tactics to make people thing they have a choice.

He was often at the theater overseeing my show. To his credit, he never interrupted or tried to overrule my authority with the cast or its actions. If he had, then we might have had this come-to-Jesus moment a lot sooner.

Instead of releasing the tirade I'd prepared the week before, I narrowed my eyes, hopefully imparting my feelings about him, and his BS suggestion, and turned back toward the theater.

He followed after a minute. The tip tap of dress shoes matching my pace alerted me to the moment when he caught up. Today he very well might have been going to the theater, so I wouldn't press further. But if I saw his face on any of my city walks, he and I would have more than words.

It was Friday, so the cast would be off. I usually spent the day working with set design and behind-the-scenes production. Gray's presence on a Friday wasn't unusual but I rarely caught a glimpse of him on days the staff took off.

He slipped through the side door at the back of the theater a few minutes after I did. This time I laid in wait. He stopped and straightened his suit jacket when he caught sight of me. In all the time he'd been watching me, I'd also been watching him. He straightened his lapels and the bottom of his coat whenever he got the tiniest bit ruffled. I was beginning to think it cute. Not today.

"We meet again so soon, Miss Vale."

"Why are you here?"

He gave me a dismissive shrug. "Protecting my investment."

"Is there some doubt about my ability as a producer or director?"

He shook his head. "No, of course not. I have a personal interest in this production."

I waited for him to elaborate but he remained silent. "Are you going to tell me what it is?"

He chuckled, an infectious laugh that pounced on my nerves, as none of this was funny. "No, of course not, where's the fun in that?"

I rolled my eyes and headed up the stairs to my office. He followed on my heels. "You may have a personal interest in the production but you have no business in my office," I said, as made it to the top, holding tight to the worn wooden bannister.

He called out from a few steps below. "I do have a question for you."

"Are you going to tell me what interest you have in my play?"

"Come to dinner with me and I might."

I stopped and twisted around to get a look at him. "Did you just ask me out on a date?"

"If you have some objection to the nomenclature we could call it a business dinner."

It took a moment for the situation to sink in. My boss—the man who owned the theater in which my first international production would show and the man who had been following me around town for weeks—had just asked me to dinner. "Is this some kind of test?"

He had the grace to look offended. "No, why would I need to test you?"

"I don't know. You've been following me and now you ask me out. I don't know what's next, a proposal of marriage or a pink slip."

"Pink slip?"

"Firing, Mr. Gray." I rolled my eyes. "Sorry, I forget my American colloquialisms sometimes don't translate."

"I have no intention of firing you."

"Then what are your expectations here?"

"To take a beautiful woman to dinner. Why do there need to be expectations?"

"Do you expect me to sleep with you?" I intended to catch him off guard with the crass question, but he didn't bat a single perfect eyelash.

"I never expect a woman to do anything. But if you want to go to bed I'm amenable."

There it was, that playboy smile I'd seen him wield with deadly accuracy several times. It was different turned on me and I realized Mr. Gray was a lot more dangerous than I'd originally believed.

"I'm sorry Mr. Gray, I don't sleep with my employers."

"You object to my employment?"

"I object to losing my job if things go south between us."

"I'm perfectly capable of separating business and pleasure."

"That's just it, Mr. Gray. I am all business and no pleasure." I turned back, climbed the rest of the way to my office, and slammed the door in his face.

That smile was imprinted in my brain. It said he got what he wanted and be damned the consequences. But I had no intention of becoming a consequence to Dorian Gray.

DORIAN

I STOOD AT THE THRESHOLD of her office. It was nothing more than a shoebox situated above the staff quarters, but she'd made it her own by bringing in her scripts and pieces of feminine décor. I caught a peek before she gave me a face full of wood. Rejection was a new sensation for me, and novelty always gave me reason to smile.

When I left home this morning and fell in step behind her, I hadn't expected to be confronted.

Perhaps I had underestimated my ability to blend in. Maybe the designer suits were too much? Regardless, I let out a sigh of relief. I'd grown weary of the subterfuge a couple weeks into the game. She turned me down now, but it wouldn't remain so. One hundred and fifty years of practice meant I usually got what I wanted, and Isobel

Vale was at the top of the list.

I headed back down the stairs to my own office toward the front of the building. Decorated in the same turn of the century style as the theater itself, it made me feel more at home than the modern accoutrements that populated some of the other offices in the building. As the owner, of course I could pick and choose.

My secretary Mina sat at her small desk in my office's antechamber. "Good morning, Mr. Gray," she offered as I swept through.

"*Bon Jour*, Mina. Any messages?"

"Not yet, Mr. Gray. But your meeting with the contractors about the theater's west wing renovations was moved to after lunch."

I gave her a nod, went into my office, and closed the door. Mina, while a sweet girl, was so young. Her presence grew tiresome for me in minutes. I could only tolerate her in small doses.

After she read that God's forsaken book about the sadist who shared my surname, she couldn't look at me without snickering for a week. It made my entire office unproductive for much longer. I'd had to ban the book and its sequels from the building. And we weren't even going to acknowledge the *other* book. Whoever deemed *The Picture of Dorian Gray* classic literature should be shot.

Thankfully the craze passed quickly, but then the movies followed.

I counted the days until I was free of the entire plot. I had no time or inclination to make games out of dominance or submission. And while my sexual exploits were eclectically varied, I'd yet to get sexual gratification out of subjugating a woman, at least in this century.

Times had changed since I was a boy. Over a hundred years had passed. Women's rights, civil rights, fashion, it was all evolution. Which was something my survival depended upon. Any woman who would remain in my life would learn quickly my tastes, or be dismissed. I liked to keep things simple and straightforward—something modern women usually appreciated.

I unbuttoned my jacket and sank into the couch across from my desk. I'd only come to work because I followed Izzy in. It became a habit. But how long had she known? There was no reason for me to be in the building today except for the contractor meeting, which wasn't until later. For now I needed to strategize a way to get that woman to agree on a date.

I closed my eyes and recalled the first moment I saw her. I frequented a café on the corner across from the theater. She'd come walking through the square clutching a newspaper. Her dress was a practical white summer thing, a tan fedora topped her short mop of blonde hair, and black sunglasses covered almost half her face. She held the American periodical under her arm and trotted through the square without so much as a glance around.

I'd thrown some money on the table and followed her down a narrow alley. She barreled through that as well, clearly with a destination in mind. As I walked, her image overlaid with another I knew so well. One I'd visualized over and over, more times than I cared to admit: Sibyl. Every inch of this woman looked exactly like her, down to the mole on her left ankle just above the strap of her shoe. I'd touched that mole, kissed that mole; seeing it again on living flesh threatened to rend me in two. Her hair, while the same soft texture, was shorter and blond, where Sibyl's had been brown. Otherwise it was as if I were looking at the same woman aged ten years. Ten whole years Sibyl never claimed.

I followed her to the solicitor I'd hired to find a producer. She exited with a smile and her sunglasses in her hand ten minutes later. Even those eyes were the same, big and dominating her face in an endearing way. The second she stepped off the curb I was torn between questioning my lawyer and following her to her next destination. My curiosity won out and I entered the solicitor's office a minute after she'd departed.

The secretary greeted me. "Mr. Gray, what a surprise. I didn't think you had an appointment today." Her French accent overtook some of the English words but I got the meaning well enough.

"May I go back?"

She gestured for me to continue and I walked through the open door at the back of the small office. Mr. Leroux sat eating a pastry, and immediately dropped it and hopped to his feet. "Mr. Gray, I wasn't expecting you."

I smiled at my old friend. "Seems to be going around, Jean-Claude."

"How may I help you, Sir?"

"The woman who left moments ago, what was her business here?"

Jean-Claude shuffled some papers on his desk before handing me three, stapled together at the corner. "She's the director and producer of *Romeo and Juliet*, soon to start casting at the theater."

Romeo and Juliet. I sighed as I glanced down at the contract. "Isobel Vale," I read aloud.

"She prefers to be called Izzy. She's an American, famous in certain Broadway circles according to her references."

I memorized her address and committed any other details I could catch to memory. If Sibyl had been reincarnated, this might be my chance to make amends. To right the wrongs committed so many years ago.

The idea unfurled inside me. Something like hope. An emotion I'd let die decades past. If I could finally be at peace, finally die, then Izzy might be the ticket to that end. And if death was off the table for me, then at the very least I might grasp atonement.

IZZY

I stared at my closed door off and on throughout the morning, half expecting Gray to barge in at any moment. He had the right, but if he possessed any knowledge about me as a person he wouldn't try it.

I went over scripts and finalized some understudies I wanted to test, and when my stomach grumbled loudly I glanced up at the clock. Noon. A good time to stop for lunch. I favored the café on the corner across from the theater. They made heavenly croissant sandwiches. Not exactly health food but I considered the almost mile I walked back and forth to work every day enough exercise to stave off the effects of too many carbs. And . . . when in Paris right?

I grabbed my wallet and phone and stuffed them into my pocket, leaving my bag as I hated lugging it around on quick trips.

The weather was warm with a nice mid-summer breeze. Any other day I'd have spent my lunch people watching outside the café. But I had more work to do and I wanted to leave earlier in the evening than usual. Which in my world meant I wanted to leave before it got dark. As I carefully navigated the cobblestones in my low heels I spotted a familiar face at my usual table. He looked different now, his jacket was thrown over the back of his chair, his dress shirt sleeves bunched up at the elbow. He held a hefty tome in one hand as he gracefully sipped an espresso, pinky out, of course.

I walked straight to the table and waited for him to look up. I cleared my throat and he finally met my eyes. The resounding zing that went through my body troubled me. It was like touching a nine volt to your tongue. "What are you doing here?"

He waved at the table with his now empty demitasse, "lunch."

"I come here for lunch."

He didn't seem fazed by my declaration. "It's the best café in the area. I know, I tried them all. You don't hold a monopoly on lunch locales." He set down his glass and gave me one of those long slow challenging looks that made me wonder whether he was arguing with me or flirting with me. Either way, I didn't like it.

I scowled at him. "Awfully suspicious though, you here eating lunch just when I come down for lunch."

"It's twelve o'clock, my dear. It's the lunch hour, that's not suspicious at all."

His focus and his gaze strayed back to the book as he spoke, and he said "my dear" in a scolding tone that should have reminded me of my grandmother, but actually made me want to hear it again.

I huffed, not very gracefully, and went inside to get food. After I placed my order I dug in my wallet for my debit card, only to find it missing. Recalling the morning's coffee, I had dropped the card into my bag instead of putting it back, a habit I'd been trying to break for some time.

My stomach rumbled loudly and I glanced out the window to the back of Gray's head. How could the back of someone's head be so perfect?

I pointed outside to where he sat as I tucked my wallet back into my pocket. "Actually, I'm joining that man out there. Put it on his tab."

A little cheeky, but if he wanted a date, he'd get a date. I walked back out and took the empty chair next to him.

He glanced up from the pages again and his perfect eyebrows rose in question. "Why, Miss Vale, are you following me?"

I rolled my eyes. "No, actually I'm joining you for lunch."

His eyes widened and he snapped the book in his hand shut. *War and Peace.* Of course.

"I was under the impression you weren't interested in me."

I gave him a sickly sweet smile. "Oh I'm not, I just forgot my debit card and decided you could buy my lunch since you want a date so badly. The least I can do is sit with you after you do."

He chuckled softly. "Touché. I reserve the right to kiss you then, when we are finished."

I leaned back and crossed my arms, trying to put as much distance as possible between us. "You reserve no such thing."

I wouldn't admit it to him, but he intrigued me. What would a millionaire playing theater director want with me? Relationships like that never worked out, and the less wealthy partner of such a pairing usually regretted the entire affair. Maybe he had a wife in England and a title he was running away from. I let out a long-suffering sigh and glanced out at the square. Watching tourists was one of my favorite things to do in the city.

His voice dragged me away from the calm I was just starting to grasp. "What if I told you that by the end of this date you'll ask me to kiss you?"

I focused back on him and his Michelangelo face, trying to replay what he was saying. When I caught up I scowled. "I'd say you need to adjust your medication."

Another of his damn smiles. "Is it a wager then?"

If he wanted to play games, I could play games with him. "What do I get if I win? Besides the pleasure of not kissing you? Which to be honest, doesn't really seem like a prize."

He smiled again. I was beginning to think he enjoyed rejection a little too much. "I promise I will stop following you around."

Ah sweet vindication. "I knew you were following me. Why?"

He shrugged. "Maybe if you win, I'll tell you. Or should we save that for our next date?"

He had my attention now, and the cocky bastard knew it. "Not doing something you shouldn't do anyway really isn't a win-win for me. You suck at the rewards thing."

His smile disappeared, thank God, and he leveled me with a serious look. Like we were about to negotiate a peace treaty between our warring countries. "What do you want then? And don't be afraid of your imagination."

I leaned in and narrowed my eyes. Mocking his business-like stare. "I want you to approve the theater upgrades so we can get our drop door." I'd been wanting one installed because I was sure the next feature I took over would need it—at least if I had anything to say about it. But the underground parts of the theater were flooded and off limits. It would take some maneuvering with the government to get it all working. My manager, one of the guys in between my level and Gray's, had basically told me to forget about it.

"And if I win?"

I leaned back now, as our faces had somehow continued to inch closer and closer during the exchange. "You'll already get a kiss. What more do you want?"

"If we are being fair here, my prize is considerably disproportionate to yours."

I shrugged. "I guess that depends on how bad you want to kiss me. She says to her stalker."

He chuckled and shifted in his chair to smooth out his perfectly tailored trousers. "How about if I win, we go on a real date? You let me do this correctly."

The waitress chose the perfect moment to sit my sandwich on the table between us. He pointed to my innocent lunch. "Case in point."

I glared, but scooted across the concrete to get closer to my food. "Were you a lawyer in another life?"

Something dark passed over his features like a cloud blocking out the sunlight. Gone as fast as it arrived.

"I'm just very adamant about getting what I want. Call it a character flaw. And a sandwich during daylight hours isn't a proper date."

I nibbled on the edge of the turkey poking out of the flakey crust as he watched me. With him here, I didn't know if I could sit and eat. I wasn't bad at putting food in my mouth, but there really wasn't an elegant way to eat a sandwich the size of your face.

He chuckled. "Don't worry about me. I'll read until you finish." He picked up the book and slid his fingers into the gap made by his bookmark at the top. Bonus points for not bending the corners.

I quickly chewed and swallowed. "Wait. I do have a question for you."

He froze and closed the book again. Instead of asking he sat patiently waiting. I didn't know how to say what I needed to say without offending him. Not that it usually stopped me but he was sort of paying me, and I needed my job to stay in Paris.

I took a deep breath and decided to just ask. "What do you want with me?"

I almost expected him to play the question off like a joke, or make up some excuse as to why he'd been following me. Part of me wanted him to do that, give me a normal rational explanation as to why he, of all people, would be interested in me.

Instead of making light of my question, he shuffled his book and my plate toward the middle of the table and grabbed the edge of my chair just outside my thighs. The pressure of his thumbs against my knees was intense, and it felt almost like he'd placed his entire hand on me. I swallowed against the sparks prickling up my skin from the contact. It was too familiar. His touch was too familiar. The look he was leveling me with was too familiar. And damn him to hell I wanted more.

He slid the chair, loudly and obnoxiously, across the pitted ground toward him until my knees sat closed on the inside of his, spread wider. He was either about to give me the best kiss of my life or scold me, and I didn't know which I wanted more.

"I'm only going to say this once," his tone was hard edged like the rough concrete he'd just pulled me across. "I like you, Isobel. I want to be more than friends with you. I don't care if I'm technically your boss and you're technically my employee."

Each word made those sparks move faster until my skin felt like it was vibrating under his scrutiny. I realized if I lightened the mood now it would likely offend him.

"Mr. Gray," I began.

He shook his head. "Dorian, please."

I stopped and stared at him. "Your name is Dorian Gray? Why didn't I notice that before?"

He met my eyes and I realized I had done exactly what I'd just instructed myself not to—made light of the moment between us. Anger simmered in his eyes and I pushed myself back on track. "We'll ignore that for now, Dorian. What I want to know is why you've been following me. I've noticed for weeks. Not exactly a good way to win a date."

His hands tightened on the edge of the chair and it caused his thumbs to flick alongside my knee caps. I didn't think he realized he was doing it but the movement still ignited my skin there. Who knew knees could be so sensitive?

"I don't want to worry you. But someone *has* been following you. Someone who isn't me. I've been following you both to make sure you stay safe."

Alarm wrenched through me. I knew that someone was following me but I'd always assumed it was just him, I'd never considered it could be someone else. Then realization dawned. I was in a foreign country, away from anyone I knew back at home. There was only one person who would have the balls to put a guard on me.

I leaned back and held up a finger to stop anything else he was about to say. He sat back and froze. "What is it?"

"May I borrow your cell phone?"

He didn't ask questions, something I liked in a man, and reached into the jacket hanging off of his chair. He handed me his phone, open to the dial screen. I wondered what would be in his text messages.

I hit the number I had been forced to learn by heart and waited for it to ring. It took three rings for a click and I spoke clearly into the line. "Juliet Alpha Kilo Echo." Then I hung up.

Gray sat back in his chair now with his hands crossed over his flat belly. "Dare I ask?"

Exactly ten seconds passed and the phone rang in my hand. I answered with: "Jake, I'm going to kill you."

"Now, is that anyway to greet your brother?"

"My brother who is about to be ball-less. Call off your guard or I'll come up with some scheme like I did in Budapest, and then you'll have to explain it to your superiors."

His warm familiar laugh came down the line and even though I was pissed at him, I reveled in that sound. His being a Navy SEAL meant I never got to see him. I missed him, even when I wanted to throw something at his head.

"I only did it for your protection."

"I can protect myself. Call him off or you will regret it."

Some shuffling came through the line. "I love you, Sis. Gotta go."

I handed the phone back to Gray. "It won't be a problem anymore."

I watched as a nondescript man stood up from one of the far tables and headed in the opposite direction. "Thank you for playing. Better luck next time." I called out.

I let out a long sigh and sat back to focus on my date once again. "Now that you have no excuse to follow me anymore, what are you going to do now?"

DORIAN

This woman had more fire than Sibyl ever did. Over the course of my week's surveillance I learned a lot about her. But the heat that burned from the inside out to touch others—I hadn't gotten to witness that until this morning. I had thought it a fluke, but now, face to face with the woman I realize that no, this was all her. Fire and grace, and an unwillingness to give in. Despite the era into which I was born, I found it highly erotic.

Some said women who knew their own minds were dangerous. I disagreed. A woman who knew her mind, and her worth, was intoxicating.

She cleared her throat and I realized my thoughts had been wandering to the past. "My apologies."

Her face flushed a pretty pink. "It's fine just stop looking at me like that."

"Like what?"

"Like I'm more than an employee."

I leaned out, about to pull her in again for another lesson but she stalled my hands, placing her small ones on the outside of my own. They were chilled slightly but the touch sent a heat through me I hadn't felt in years.

"I think we just had this conversation."

She leaned in and pulled her hands into her lap. "No, we had a lecture. You told me how you wanted it and didn't give me the chance to offer an opinion."

Fair point. "Very well, what is your opinion on the matter, Miss Vale?"

"Do you actually want to know, or are you going to do that playboy billionaire thing where you declare something to be and suddenly the universe aligns against the poor unsuspecting female you set your sights on?"

I chuckled. She was funny. Maybe Sibyl had been funny too, and I never took the time to notice. "I promise your opinion will be considered with appropriate weight."

"That sounds like something a billionaire playboy would say."

I didn't respond to her taunts but waited instead for her answer.

She raked her eyes over my face and body, and I'd never felt more on display. I sat up straighter, which caused a little tick of a smile to appear at the corner of her mouth.

"I don't want to date you, Gray. You're technically my boss, and while you're very attractive I can't put aside my personal work ethic."

My heart hit my feet and shattered like a boulder into a pile of rubble. Of course I wasn't going to force her to do anything. But part of me had hoped my charm or appeal might at least give me the opportunity.

"Is there anything I can do to change your mind?"

She shook her head and gave me a sad soft smile, the kind reserved for deathbeds and christenings. Definitely not the reaction I wanted from her. Not the smile I wanted from her.

I nodded and stood up, unable to remain under her scrutiny once she'd made her opinion so very plain. "Of course. I'll not bother you again."

"And you'll stop following me?"

I threw some bills on the table, slipped my arms into my coat, and buttoned it, all without meeting her eyes. The rejection stung. In fact, I don't think I'd ever felt this particular mix of humiliation and sadness. Once I was put together and glued on the face I showed the world, I gave her my own version of the deathbed smile and a little bow. "Of course."

I walked away without a word but when I reached the middle of the square a hand clasped my shoulder. Izzy grabbed me and held out the book I'd left on the table. I took it and met her eyes, unsure what she could see there, unsure what I could and couldn't hide when I was around her.

She leaned in and whispered, "I'm not going to ask to kiss you but I will give you this as a parting gift."

The scent of her surrounded me as well as the tang of chicken salad and soft croissant. The coffee on my own breath. I swallowed, unsure what she was aiming at. When she leaned in to place a soft kiss on my cheek only an inch beside my mouth, I decided if I only got one shot at this I might as well make the most of it.

Instead of letting her end it there I wrapped my hands around her cheeks, looked deep into those blue eyes and waited a hair's breadth of a second for her to pull away if she wanted.

It was a new kind of relief when she remained, and I didn't allow her a second chance. I kept my eyes open, watching her emotions war in a mix of curiosity and reluctance. When I pressed my lips to hers, they cleared into something far more delightful.

As she softened to me I gave in, closed my eyes, and savored the feel of her soft skin on mine. It lasted a second until I released her and stepped back. She stood stock still, her hands still where they'd lifted to clutch my forearms, eyes closed, lips open and freshly flushed.

"Good Day, Miss Vale," I said, before tucking my book under my arm and heading back to my office. At the very least, I'd given her something to think about. At the most, I'd been given a memory to cherish until maybe, in another life, we might play this game again.

I ignored everyone until I was in my office, the door shut tight. Then I let the mask drop away and sat unmoving on the couch. The doctors called it depression. The way I felt hollow all the time, mostly feeling absolutely nothing, until something could spark me and I would feel human again for a short while. It never took long for it to return. They wanted me on some sort of medication, and while I wasn't against pharmaceuticals, I had no idea what and how my body would react to anything. I wasn't exactly a normal man.

Instead I'd practice being normal and when I was alone I could break the mask and tell myself it was ok not to feel anything.

Izzy had changed that recently. It would only take a glimpse of her to bring me to life for a week at a time. After that kiss I should have been walking on clouds, and yet the idea of never doing it again crushed any happiness I'd garnered for those brief seconds.

The macabre part of me wondered if this was how it was meant to go in the past. Maybe Sibyl was never supposed to meet me, or fall in love. Maybe if I hadn't been selfish and pushed her she would have lived out her life, perfectly oblivious to me and my dark desires.

If I'd have been a stronger man, maybe I would have let her. Even as I tried to convince myself I knew it was all a lie. I was as powerless against Sibyl in all her glory as I was against Izzy now. All she had to do was say the word and I'd crawl at her feet.

Was I seeking forgiveness from Izzy for my mistakes with Sibyl? Maybe. What was so wrong with that? It wasn't as if she'd ever know, ever understand how much I needed to make amends for my sins, or how much I'd done over the years in the attempt.

I glanced up at the bookshelf lining the wall behind my desk. It was basically the only solace I had in this world that I seemed unable to quit. I got up and placed *War and Peace* on the shelf carefully between Proust and Kafka, the spines flush and straight. I'd already read it at least a hundred times. Some new material might be in order.

I hopped on the computer and scrolled through the wish list on my favorite book retailer, but before I could pinpoint something a light knock came at the door.

I didn't have any more appointments and I only returned to the office because I didn't want Izzy to think her rejection of me hurt as a bad as it did.

"Come in," I called. Then I schooled my features into my trademark look of mild curiosity and billionaire savoir faire.

The door popped open and then inched farther as Izzy stepped inside. "So this is the bat cave huh?"

"Can I help you, Miss Vale?"

She cleared her throat and gestured at the chair across the desk. "May I sit?"

"Of course, please."

"I saw that you approved the updates. You did that earlier, before I even proposed it as a prize in that game, didn't you?"

I shrugged. "Maybe. Or maybe I really think it needs an update."

She let out a long-suffering sigh and measured me across the desk. I could feel her eyes on me, going over every single inch. Fortunately, years at this meant she'd never find a hair out of place. "Mr. Gray, would you like to accompany me for a drink this evening?"

I had to keep my joy, which was threatening to choke me, from my tone. "Why Miss Vale, do you think that entirely appropriate? I am your boss, after all."

She stood up and tossed a paper ball at my chest before heading toward the door. Her hair stood up on one side and she'd dropped some sandwich on her blouse to join the coffee stain. And yet, even in her perpetual state of disarray, I wanted her.

"I'll pick you up at seven, Gray. Don't make me wait."

IZZY

I CHECKED MY HAIR IN the mirror one final time. The golden strands, and the too-dark roots, sat perfectly. The entire evening seemed to be falling into place. I was able to leave work early, no creepy strangers following me home. Then the shop around the corner had my favorite wine, my eyeliner wings were on point, and now my pixie hair sat artfully disarrayed around my head in that sexy bedhead vibe I'd been failing at for a month.

One swipe of lipstick and I headed out the door, clutch and heels in hand. I'd put them on at the bar to give Gray something to look at. The sky-high royal blue velvet pumps made my legs look like they never stopped.

The warm night air bolstered me as I headed to the taxi on the curb. I climbed inside and gave directions to the driver, while attempting to ignore the way the scent of my peach blossom perfume mixed with the curry the driver must have been eating before he picked me up.

As we pulled up outside Gray's building it occurred to that me the man probably had his own car service. No. I squared my shoulders and climbed out of the vehicle. His secretary had given me directions, and now the doorman held the door open wide for me.

"*Qui êtes-vous ici pour voir, Madmoiselle?*"

My French being a little terrible I caught about half of what he said. "*Monsuier*, Gray?"

"Yes, of course," the man said in perfect English, not even an accent.

He went behind a tall desk and picked up the phone. Some words were exchanged in French and then he hung up. "Mr. Gray will be down momentarily."

I nodded and stepped away from the counter. Part of me was sad I wouldn't get to see his apartment. Another part of me was happy the temptation wouldn't be present.

I'd avoided thinking about that kiss all day. But now that I was about to see him again there was no stopping the way it played in my mind like a movie reel set to loop. He'd taken the liberty, and damn it, I wanted him to do it again. It was the only reason I'd asked him out after my speech about dating the boss.

Chemistry like that couldn't be faked, and I'd spent a lot of years with duds—long enough to know how badly a relationship can go without it. I wished like hell he wasn't my boss though. It would make wanting to use him for sex so much less abashing. Or at the very least, it would make me feel less guilty about it.

Instead of waiting to do it in the bar, I stripped off my flats, picked them up, and folded them into my clutch. I glanced up to catch the doorman staring, a bemused expression on his face.

I shrugged and slid on the heels without a single wobble. "They hurt to walk on the cobblestones."

He inclined his head and focused on the elevator. It dinged, the gleaming doors slid open with a swish, and out stepped Gray like he was shooting a cologne ad or something. I almost wanted to sigh in frustration.

He wore black dress pants, a white shirt folded to the elbow, a navy tie, and a vest that cut a tight figure.

I looked him over and felt entirely underdressed in my skinny jeans, pink velvet cami, and heels. "It's ok that you decided not to dress up," I offered.

He froze in the middle of adjusting a sleeve at his elbow, a look of alarm crossing his features for a split second before clearing. "Very funny, Miss Vale."

"I suppose you can call me Izzy. And by the way, Dorian, don't think for one minute that we're not going to be talking about your name."

He held out his elbow and I allowed him to help me into the taxi idling at the curb. Once I was settled, he climbed in on the opposite side and I gave him brownie points for not mentioning the smell, the taxi in general, or the fact that he probably could have ordered a limo or something to take us out.

"You look beautiful tonight, Izzy," he said from his very far away side of the car. I could barely catch the edge of something that smelled warm and spicy emanating from him. Like cinnamon or cloves. I wanted to move closer but he already had too much power in this relationship—between me telling him I wouldn't date him, then letting him kiss me, and me asking him out. I didn't need to be throwing myself on him in the back of a taxi on top of it.

I forced myself to stare out the window at the passing pedestrians as we made our way through narrow streets before I responded. "Thank you. So do you."

I stole a glance his way in time to see the corner of his mouth lift the tiniest bit. An unguarded gesture that measured high on the reaction meter for him—the man of many masks.

The taxi stopped outside my favorite bar and I handed the driver cash before Gray could even retrieve his wallet. He didn't put up a fuss though and followed me onto the sidewalk.

"I don't think I've ever been taken out by a woman before." He mused, and slipped his hands into his pockets.

"No?" I gestured to the thin brick building behind us and he followed me inside. A haze of smoke filled the dark room and I claimed my favorite table in the very back of the long narrow bar. It was perfect for people watching, and my friend who tended the bar usually kept it empty with a reserved sign when she was knew I was coming. I grabbed the plastic card, turned it to the side, and slid into the curve of the oval-shaped booth. Dorian followed, keeping a respectable distance between us.

A soft jazz tune played quiet and slow from outdated speakers in each corner of the bar. And before I could even warm up my first piece of conversation, the other regular bartender brought two of my usual.

Gray took the tall pint of beer without a word.

"You're pretty accommodating for a millionaire." I said as he took a sip.

He swallowed and turned to face me. "I promise you I'm not always acquiescing. But when I want something I can be."

Heat trickled up my neck and into my ears but I didn't flinch, maintaining eye contact, as I sipped my own beer. Once I'd swallowed I swiveled to face him as well. "Noted."

"So this is a local haunt of yours?"

"Didn't you find that out while you were stalking me?"

He shook his head and picked up the sign. "No, but they seem to know you and your usual routines."

"My friend works here so I do spend a lot of time here. Once rehearsals start back up I don't think I'll be around much."

"And how are you liking…?"

I held up my hand. "Hold it, Gray. We are not talking about work."

"What would you like to talk about then?"

I let out a sigh and scooted an inch closer so I could hear better over the music and the other patrons. He must have taken it as permission and did the same, so only a few inches separated us on the black vinyl. "I want to talk about that kiss."

He let out a soft snort that even I had to strain to hear. "You really do like to jump right in, don't you?"

"Do you prefer women with more guile and games?"

He raked his eyes across my features and leaned back so his shoulder pressed into the backrest of the booth. "No, I have no enjoyment for games when it comes to romance."

I moved closer, my knee touching his now, feeling bolder between the darkness and the beer. "I hope you have some room in your life for games."

His face changed. It wasn't exactly the playboy mask I was used to seeing, but his lips and eyes were definitely squarely in the mischief column. "I am open to any suggestions you might have, Izzy."

I took another sip of my beer and let the condensation from the frozen glass run down my fingers. He watched me, his eyes hooded, lips half turned in a smile. Once my fingers were chilled I put them on his full bottom lip, tracing it with my fingertip. He opened his mouth and took it inside. His tongue swiped against my fingerprint and created a direct line to my panties. I let go and tried to mask the arousal no doubt written all over my face.

"I'm sorry," he whispered.

I shook my head. "No, you have nothing to apologize for."

He reached out and pulled me in so we sat side by side, hip to hip, and he wrapped his arm around me. The world looked different inside the curve of his embrace. Like I'd been peering at the universe through a porthole in a submarine that had just surfaced for the first time.

Something had shifted and I couldn't figure out when. Was it the moment he kissed me, and I decided I'd have him? Even if it ended badly. Even *when* it ended badly. Even when he'd likely demolish my heart.

I felt the need to break the tension, to shine some light on the shadows that were slowly creeping in. "You do know I plan on using you for sex, right?"

My mouth did that sometimes, ran away without my brain.

He jerked against me and turned my head with his fingers to look up at his face. I couldn't read the expression there now. Not another mask, but not the same look as before. This one was as inscrutable as his playboy mask but there was an edge of vulnerability to it.

"Is that all you're offering?" he asked so quietly I could barely hear him.

"For now."

He shrugged and lifted his arm away from my shoulders. "Then I'll take what I can get. I'm hopeful I can change your mind. As you noticed earlier, my powers of persuasion are unmatched."

"Was that a joke, Gray?" I laughed despite the absurdity of the entire situation. "We are on the same page though right? I don't want you thinking you own me or anything."

He leaned in, and that spicy scent wrapped me up in heat. When his lips stopped—licking distance from my own—I could see the match waiting to strike against the roughened edges of my need for him. "I'd never presume to own you. That would be like trying to own the sun. An easy way to get scorched."

There was a question there that he wasn't asking. "But?" I said, shifting to get closer. He reached up and gripped my chin, keeping me too close and too far at the same time.

Fucking hell this man knew how to tease a woman.

"But, we should discuss some things."

I couldn't help it, I squirmed in his hands. Worse yet, I felt no shame in it.

He leaned past my face to press his lips almost fully against my ear, leaving only a breath's worth of space between us. His exhale heated my skin and tickled the fine hairs on my face before his words struck that hovering match. Each syllable a fan to the building flame.

"I will never allow you to be at the mercy of your emotions. I will use them, you will enjoy them, and we will dominate them."

DORIAN

A BEAUTIFUL WOMAN IN MY embrace is the end to an enjoyable evening. An experience I had forgone for probably a decade. But a woman trembling, needing, aching in my arms is some kind of biblical.

I didn't want to do this here. The bar wasn't crowded or dirty in the least, but it was still public. I wanted Izzy all to myself. "Would it be presumptive of me to pay the bill and call my car?" I whispered, still trailing my lips teasingly around the arches of her delicate ear.

She swallowed, loud and heavy and wet, before answering. "No, not presumptuous since I'm three seconds from climbing into your lap."

I couldn't help the surge of pride that burst through me. Moments like this were definitely something I appreciated about the modern era.

Women who took what they wanted from a lover without compunction. She didn't need to ask me twice. I sent a text to my driver, climbed out of the booth, and dropped a couple bills on the table. Once I'd paid, she handed me her bag. I took it without thinking and then she glanced down to the very obvious tent of my pants.

I couldn't care less if the entire country knew what she did to me. But in case she might be embarrassed, I carried her bag out into the dark street to shield my arousal.

My driver pulled up in a black town car before I could attempt conversation with a raging hard on. I opened the door for her and slid in behind her.

She shifted in the seat so her thighs aligned with mine. "Your driver got here very fast."

I didn't bother with the seatbelt or the side-by-side business, and lifted her off the leather into my lap. She took the hint and straddled my thighs.

She wiggled down so our bodies aligned in that absolute way. "Oh that's better."

I wrapped my hands around her to cup the shape of her ample hips. Before I had time to process it all, she had me flat against the back of the seat, hips swiveling against my cock, trailing teeth and lips and wet heat down the side of my neck. My mind blanked and I gave in to the need for her. The tingle in my appendages, the raging blood in my dick. If I weren't so practiced at playing a gentleman, I'd have ripped open her jeans and fucked her right there in the back of my car for the whole world to witness.

Those long-dormant depraved depths of me almost demanded it. *Almost.*

She reached into my hair and gripped the strands tight, pulling them before pressing her hips up to take my mouth.

Fuck, I could smell her arousal. That promise of sweaty sheets and a warm wet entrance. I reached out, clutching her as tightly to me as possible. Everything. All of it. I wanted every single inch of her body against mine. Those throaty sighs she made as our lips molded together, tongues seeking permission and battling for domination.

She kissed like she lived. With heat and fire, and a little bite.

When she released my hair from her vice-like fingers she pulled away from my lips, trailing her nails down my chest. I could barely feel it through my clothes, but the promise of it, the violence of it, was enough to set me trembling for her.

"How far?" she asked. That was it. As if forming full sentences was too much right now.

I glanced out the window to clear my brain and saw the last turn toward my building.

"Seconds," I whispered, pulling her in for another kiss. A little more. Just a little taste to tide me over until I got her inside.

The car stopped and we both reached for the door handle. She laughed and climbed off me and out the door. I followed as close as I was able until we reached the elevator.

As it climbed the ten stories to the top floor I cursed my penthouse for the first time in my life. The seven-by-seven-foot space held more sexual tension than I think the safety code permitted.

The gleaming stainless steel door slid open achingly slowly. We stood in front of my flat and I tried to maintain my composure while I unlocked the door to let her in.

After I locked it again, I turned to face her. "Do you want a drink?"

She tilted her head and lowered her eyebrows to give me a purely feminine look that even I recognized, having been off women for a decade, before the slow shake of her head. "Do you really think I came over here for a drink?"

Now that we'd both taken a breather, the clarity of the situation was starting to filter in. My lust-addled mind pinged warnings through the haze like a lighthouse in a dense fog. This was meant to be my second chance with her, not a booty call or whatever ridiculous name they'd given one night stands in this century. Albeit people usually didn't do one night stands with their employers.

"Stop," she said, forceful and clear.

I froze and met her eyes. "What?"

She ambled closer and began to slip the buttons of my vest through their opposing holes. "Whatever it is that you're thinking about right now. Just stop. I can see the gears whirring about in that head of yours. I'm not letting your brain cock-block me."

Cock block wasn't a term I'd picked up this decade but the meaning was clear. "I just don't want you to think this is all I want from you."

Once she finished the buttons of my vest she stripped it off my shoulders and let it drop in a soft puddle on the floor. Then she started on my dress shirt with a single-mindedness I found both erotic and impressive.

"I was very clear at the bar. I'm the one using *you* for sex."

She finished there and stripped the shirt away to join the vest on the floor. When she encountered my T-shirt she stopped. "Really? How much clothing is necessary for a few drinks?"

I shrugged. "I have to protect my honor."

She rewarded me with a snort chuckle that warmed me to my toes. Then she yanked the hem of my shirt out of my pants hard enough I almost stumbled for balance. "I can remove my own clothing."

Another sexy grin. "I know, but I like undressing a man. It's like opening a Christmas present to find Santa brought you everything you wanted and more."

Next, the white cotton was up and over my head faster than I'd have been able to manage.

As she bee lined for my belt buckle I halted her fingers before they could work the brass closure. "This entire situation is severely disproportionate."

She laughed this time, a loud guffaw that echoed off the hardwood and granite of my home, before stepping back and kicking off her heels. With three less inches of height she stared up at me now. And she made sure to lock her eyes to mine as she twisted her camisole off over her head to drop it on the floor.

And in a microsecond the raging inferno relit. She wasn't wearing a bra. Standing in my entryway with only a pair of denim blue jeans between her wet flesh and my body, I knew I wasn't going to be able to stop myself.

I reached out and tugged her to me by the waistband of her jeans.

She came easily enough, going straight for my belt buckle again. She opened it before I got her button and zipper down. Why were women's fastenings backwards? A fact I'd forgotten, or overlooked, in the last ten years.

She let my trousers go and shimmied out of her jeans to reveal a black lace pair of boy shorts. I froze and stared. When she cleared her throat, I finished taking off my trousers to pool in the minefield by the door.

I pulled her into my body and wrapped my hands around her waist. Her skin was so soft and warm, the faint scent of peaches let loose by her clothing. As naked skin met naked skin I stopped thinking again, my mind going blank to everything but the sensation.

I was about to drop to my knees in front of her, but she beat me to it, and pulled my cock from my black boxer briefs before I could utter a word to stop her.

"Why, Mr. Gray, you were holding out on me," she joked before situating herself to take the length of me into her mouth. Watching it was an out of body experience. I could see the way her tongue lapped at the underside of my sensitive flesh while at the same time feeling the heat and pleasure that accompanied the action as if from far away.

Then I slammed back to my body and the sensations were

brighter, harder, and stronger than before. Her mouth with its oh-so-wet heat gripped me, tight and demanding. She used her hand to cup the wet flesh as it left her mouth to continue the pleasure.

The carnality of her fucking me with her face broke a control inside me I didn't think I'd be able to mend. I reached out and gripped the soft bit of hair I could fist in my hands at the nape of her neck. She gave me a moan of approval and it was all the permission I would seek. I held her head tight and took the pleasure she had been offering for myself.

She wrapped her hands around my hips and held onto me. The tips of her sharp little nails dug in. I watched the scene still so far in the moment I couldn't force my brain to take over and release her.

I fucked her face hard, fast, brutally, and there wasn't a bit of me that could stop it, even as hot wet tears sprang from the corners of her eyes, spreading her mascara in a black swath down her cheeks.

Seconds, minutes, hours, days. I didn't know how much time passed. It was only me and her and the pleasure of her mouth gripping me. My climax surged forward like the last firecracker in a barrel. It sparked and I broke free from her, pulling away to milk my seed into my own hand. I shuddered and shook and shattered from the force of it. Now clear of my body's demands, I straightened again, and my brain went into overdrive as I faced her, expecting censure.

She stood against the wall in her black lace boy shorts, mascara and tears streaming down her cheeks. Her hair stood up in little spikes and whirls all over her head, and lipstick ran down her chin and smeared up to her nose. Every part of her pale skin had a pink flush I wanted to trace with my teeth.

She'd been on her knees for me seconds ago and now she stood like she owned the world and me with it.

I grabbed the T-shirt and wiped my hands of the mess I'd made. She watched me, never moving to wipe the marks of me from her skin. My mind warred. Did I sink down and return the favor, or grovel and apologize for using her so carelessly?

I was in the middle of the second option when she stepped across discarded clothing and gripped the back of my neck to pull me down. It was a clear sign as to what she wanted, and enough to entice worship from a man like me.

It wasn't smooth or graceful or perfect as I'd trained myself to be for over 150 years. I yanked at her panties and they stuck at her knees. She had to help me pull them from her feet. Then I tried to taste her standing, and I couldn't get enough of her wet heat in my mouth.

I stood, picked her up, and tossed her onto the chaise end of my black leather sectional.

"Comfy," she commented before spreading her legs wide. I dragged her by the hips to the edge and got my first good look at everything I hungered for.

"Oh, Sibyl," I whispered before leaning in for my first true taste.

Izzy's hand caught me by the forehead, her flat palm pushing me away. The error I'd made hit me with the force of a brick wall, squeezing the air from my lungs and pressing my heart into the tight closure of my throat. Shit. Fuck. Damn and hellfire.

She closed her legs and tucked them around me to stand. I reached out and caught nothing but air. "Izzy," I whispered.

I didn't have experience with this. How did a man fix such a wrong?

She dressed with impressive speed and pulled flat shoes from the depths of her purse. I didn't speak as she removed a tissue and cleaned her face. I watched, fearing a rebel tear might spring forth. In sadness or humiliation, it didn't matter.

She closed her bag forcefully and I pushed myself off the sofa to stand. "Please don't go."

When she finally met my eyes I could see the anger simmering there, waiting for a lash to wield. It turned out she didn't need one.

"A little advice for you, Gray. Don't say another woman's name during sex. Just a little tip from one fuck buddy to another."

IZZY

I stepped out onto the street and the first thought that filtered through was: that didn't go as planned.

My attempts at sex rarely did. I should have known this would be the same. It was my fault for thinking differently. And it was his fault for being all charming and smooth and convincing me that he might be worth the hassle.

Angry and humiliated didn't begin to cover my emotional spectrum. At least the storm of emotions replaced the simmering under my skin that his body caused.

A tiny part of me was pissed for leaving. He'd have likely made up for his mistake several times with his body. There could have been amazing shower sex. I love good shower sex.

I shook my head and raised my chin, about to try to find a taxi. Before I could hit the send button on my phone, a black limo pulled up and the same driver from earlier stepped out.

I hoped I'd done a decent job of cleaning my face. "Uh, hello again."

"Hello, Miss."

I looked him up and down, from the polished high shine of his oxfords to the crisp jacket over a smooth ironed white shirt. "I hope he pays you well."

He smiled and opened the back door. "He pays me very well, Miss."

I climbed in, but hunkered near the door as we took off. Sitting too close to the middle reminded me of earlier and that threatened to amp up the arousal and the fury.

I pressed my forehead to the side of the glass and huffed a cloud out to fog it. I'd only gotten through a few puffs before we stopped again.

The driver returned to open my door, but I beat him to it, already waving a goodbye before he reached the handle.

Once I'd made it into my apartment, I stripped my clothing and padded straight to the shower. Nothing washed away regret like scalding hot water.

I sat down on the slowly heating tile and leaned my head back, considering my situation. I needed to take stock of the facts. My boss was hot as hell; we'd almost had sex before he addressed my vagina by another woman's name. I'd run out after an angry—and deserved—word of reproach.

Yup. That covered it.

I wanted to figure out how I felt about everything but right now all I felt was turned on and unfulfilled. I'd been better and I'd been worse.

I washed my hair sitting cross legged in the bottom of the shower. When it was time to get the shampoo out, my legs and hips ached from sitting on the hard surface so long. The water was already starting to run cold.

I dressed in the oldest, most worn T-shirt I owned. My brother Jake's Navy SEAL tee—the one he brought back after his acceptance to the program.

With my brother's comforting arms wrapped around me, I climbed under the duvet and snuggled into the down comforter. Gray could wait until tomorrow.

Bang Bang Bang.

I blinked my eyes open to the dark room. Dots of light littered the wall from buildings, cars, and lamps outside. I blinked again, thinking maybe I'd heard the noise from the neighbors. I settled back in, and the banging restarted.

BANG BANG BANG.

I let out a groan disguised as a whine and shifted the warm covers back.

BANG BANG BANG.

"For fuck's sake," I said. Then louder, "Hold on, I'm coming."

I shuffled across the heated hardwood to the door and jerked it open to the too-bright hallway light. Dorian Gray in the flesh.

"We are not talking about this right now Gray, go away."

I moved to shut the door but he blocked it with his hand at the center, halting its progress.

"I'm not here to talk about that, but we will, I assure you. I'm here because of the theater."

Adrenaline shot through my body, bringing me fully awake. "What about the theater?"

"You have to come in with me."

I groaned and turned to the bedroom to put on pants. My boobs were barely big enough to warrant a bra so I just left my brother's sleep shirt on and threw on a pair of worn black leggings with wool flat boots.

He stared around my entrance as I grabbed my keys and walked out the door without a word, not even bothering to hold it for him. It took a few minutes for him to fumble with it and follow me out.

Maybe this retribution thing would be more fun than I thought. I wondered how far I could push it before he called me on it.

I took the stairs in a sharp right and he skidded past the door toward the elevator only to turn around and head back.

When we got downstairs his faithful driver stood with the door open. If it weren't an emergency I would have walked to the theater rather than ride with him. Even if the sun had barely begun to wash away the darkness.

"You haven't been to bed have you, Jeeves?"

His brows drew together and his lips pursed in thought. "My name's not Jeeves."

"Well," I climbed into the car and leaned out to a huff from Gray. "You didn't tell me your name so..."

Gray answered and shooed the driver to the front. "His name's Michael."

He settled into the back opposite me on another seat, thankfully.

"Nice to meet you, Michael." I shouted. I got a little jolt of pleasure to watch Gray close his eyes in quiet annoyance.

"So what's going on?"

Gray opened his eyes and focused on me again. The image of his head thrown back in pleasure flashed through my mind. I shook it off and gave him my best professional disinterested face. He matched it with his playboy mask. "I had some renovations going on the west wing. They have to work at night due to city ordinances."

"Okay...?"

"Well, they were in there working tonight and found more than expected, mold everywhere. The entire cast dressing quarters are now cut off from us."

I swore loud and viciously. When I looked up Gray's eyes were a little wide.

"Never mind that. You know how damn picky those actors are."

He nodded. "Yes, very particular."

Which meant we would lose our starring cast if we didn't play this right.

"What can we do?" I shook my hands and leaned forward. Between missing my morning coffee and the events of last night my brain wasn't firing the right way.

Gray shrugged. "You're the producer. I figured you would be able to think of a solution. I don't handle the actors. That is by design."

I snorted. "Coward."

He held his hands up in surrender. "Guilty."

To be fair, our actors were some of the best in Paris and they were divas accordingly. "Ok. Do you have a budget for a solution?"

He narrowed his eyes and for the first time I noticed he wasn't wearing a suit. He had on blue plaid pajama pants and a black Ramones T-shirt. I found it oddly sexy before I girded myself with memories of the previous night. No way in hell was I making that mistake again.

"Within reason."

I could fix anything with a large enough budget. And emotional actors could always be persuaded with enough space, free food, and easy access for complaint. "Okay, then I think I can spin it."

I held my hand out. "I need your phone."

He didn't hesitate, simply pulled it from his pocket and slapped it into my open grasp.

I dialed the only number I knew that could help in this situation.

"Pierre," A pause. "Yes, I know what time it is. Don't worry, it will be worth your while. I need you at the theater as soon as possible."

He mumbled something in French that I wasn't good enough to

catch. "Juuuust get there."

I hung up and handed the phone back.

"Friend of yours?"

I shrugged and sat back into the leather with a sigh. We stopped outside the theater with a jerk and I got out as Michael reached the door again. "Too slow Mikey. Gotta keep up."

He laughed and said something I didn't catch as I raced inside and up to my office. Gray followed, close on my heels.

"Stop flirting with my driver."

I threw myself into the chair behind my desk and shuffled papers around for the list of the cast members' contact information. "What, are you jealous, Gray?"

He sat on the edge of the worn brown leather club chair across from the desk and surveyed the organized chaos before answering. "Yes, actually."

I snorted and gave him a look. It said "really?"

He looked sheepish for a moment, his eyes saying, "I know I screwed it up."

We didn't have the conversation but I knew it was coming if I didn't do something to stop it.

I tossed the paper across the desk and it floated down to graze his knee before sinking to the floor. He picked it up. "What do you want me to do with this?"

"Start making calls. Those actors will respond more nicely to you than to me changing up the rehearsal schedule."

To his credit he flipped his phone over in his hand and was about to dial. "Wait, what do I tell them?"

I took a deep breath and sat back, blowing the air out my nose in one long exhale. "Tell them the renovations are running long and you don't want their creative genius influenced by the chaos of the theater. We are moving rehearsals to studio space for the time being."

"And what if we don't get it fixed in time for the performance?"

"I have a plan for that too."

He shook his head and dialed the first number. I checked the clock. 5 AM. I needed coffee like I needed oxygen.

Instead of hunting down my assistant this early, I gathered myself up and headed toward the door, absolutely not looking at Gray as I passed.

"Where are you going?" he asked, covering the bottom of the phone with his hand.

I opened the door and stepped out. "Coffee." Then closed it before he could respond.

Being near him now messed with my head. Both the memory of

the smooth charming operator and the awed lover took up space in my brain, and I couldn't place him in one single category that would satisfy me. Employer. Boss. Man who pays my salary. Those were good solid categories I should stick with. The memory of his dick in my mouth made it hard to keep him contained in that tiny very economical box, though.

I walked to my favorite corner cafe, and ordered an espresso. The lady handed it over and when I tried to pay, she shook her head and answered my quizzical look in broken English. "Was paid for. You have a tab."

I clutched the coffee cup tight and held it protectively against my chest. I'd never had a preemptive tab before. I wondered if this was how rich people lived. As I headed back to the theater I also wondered when he'd had time to set me up a tab at my favorite coffee shop and why.

When I got back to my office, I found him sitting, his hair sticking up in the front from his hand raking the strands as he talked on the phone. It was a sexy look for him.

No. Boss. Not sexy.

I took my seat as he hung up. "Almost done," he said, his eyes a little wide and panicky.

I couldn't help but laugh. He gave me a not-helping plea with his eyes but I wasn't going to show pity.

"So when did you find time to set up a tab across the street?"

He looked up from dialing and stopped. "I did it yesterday after we ate lunch. I realized if you and the staff went there often it made sense to start a running tab with them. They offered a discount. It keeps up morale."

So the tab wasn't for me specifically but for the staff…hmmm. "Anyway, any problems?" I asked nodding toward the phone.

"I can't reach our Juliet, but it might be too early for her."

I nodded. "Josephine is definitely not a morning person. It's why we don't start rehearsal until 11."

I sipped some more from the cup until the tension grew and began to choke the air in the room. I let out a long sigh and sat up, squaring my shoulders. "Fine. I'll let you explain about last night. But I reserve the right to forget all of this ever happened and go back to addressing you as Mr. Gray, the hot theater manager I notice from very far away."

He blinked a few times and his face changed again, another not-mask, as he sat the phone and list carefully on the edge of the desk.

"I guess I should start at the beginning."

DORIAN

I RUBBED MY SWEATY PALMS down the flannel of my pajama pants. "There really is no easy way to say this."

She swiveled her chair left to right left to right as she watched me. Her face told me she couldn't care less, but the intensity of her eyes gave her away. "Just say it."

There were very few people who knew my condition. I wasn't ready to let her in on all my secrets, but giving her the truth seemed like the only way to explain last night and keep her in my life. Maybe. If she believed me. Which was never assured when it came to revealing the truth.

The chair began to creak with her movements and I glanced back up to her face. She raised her eyebrows, waiting.

I took a deep breath and let it out slowly. I wished I were brave enough to meet her eyes as I spoke but instead I focused on the unruly stack of paper at the corner of the desk, printed in various shades of white and gray. "I was born in 1867."

The words hung there in the room, heavy and pregnant, waiting for someone to offer them a chair.

I glanced over to look at her, one quick flick of my eyes in case I caught too much. It was the same indifferent expression she'd worn before, so I stayed there, our gazes locked now. "The book, *The Picture of Dorian Gray*, was written as revenge for a rejection of the author."

She blinked a few times in rapid succession but said nothing, betrayed nothing, gave me nothing. So I continued.

"I was in my early twenties at the time. Anyway, that part isn't important, I suppose the reason I don't look 160 years old might be the important bit."

More blinking, more waiting. I licked my suddenly dry lips and let out a shuddering exhale. "There is something wrong with my telomeres. They're the nucleotide sequence that keep..."

She continued for me, "Keep your chromosomes from deteriorating or fusing with others."

"Yes," I breathed. "How do you know what telomeres are?"

She shrugged. "I watch a lot of Discovery Channel. Go on."

I made a note to watch more Discovery Channel if the opportunity arose and she didn't throw something at me before I'd finished the story.

"Obviously for a long time I didn't know why I couldn't die, or be severely wounded. Then one day the government asked me to come in for questioning. I didn't leave for a year."

"The government held you for a year?"

I nodded. "In a nine-by-nine box. Until someone higher up in the food chair figured they could study me—and the others like me—better with our cooperation."

"Which government?" she asked.

"I'm sorry?" I understood her question but it didn't seem entirely relevant to me.

"I asked which government held you illegally for a year?"

I swallowed and tried to keep the memories of that time at bay. "The American government. They were particularly interested in military applications of my ability. But I wasn't created, I was born this way, and they quickly realized they couldn't force it on another person."

The chair creaked again and I glanced up to weigh how she was feeling. Still nothing. This woman had a poker face to rival my own. And I'd had over a hundred years of practice.

I tried to focus back on the story. "Anyway, I visit their scientists every year, as do others like me born around the world. They study us—we volunteer for this—and they tell us things we need to know."

Swivel. Swivel. "Like what?" She could have been asking what the weather looked like outside.

"Like the fact that I will probably go insane before I die horrifically."

The chair froze and she sat up. "What? They told you that?"

"My telomeres are elastic but my brain isn't. At some point, like a hard drive, it's going to overload, and that will probably be an awful experience."

She blinked and leaned toward me. Her hand jerked for a second like she might reach across the desk but she didn't. Instead she sat back again. "Okay. So who is Sibyl?"

I swallowed heavy and loud. The nerves that had started to settle took up a new tune, as if freshly plucked. "Did you read that book?"

"You mean *Fifty Shades of Grey*?" A smile flitted across her face for a flash of a second.

"Not that one. The other one."

Swivel, swivel. "No, I haven't read it."

I rubbed my knees again, shifting back and forth slightly, trying to calm myself. "Well, not all of it was lies. Some of the things were true. Obviously, my being somewhat death-challenged."

That earned me a snort and I took the confidence that came packaged with it. "Some of the more debaucherous activity actually happened. But the most important thing to me was the girl."

"Sibyl." It wasn't a question. More of a whisper, hovering in the air like an accusation.

"Yes. She was an actress. I was infatuated with her and she with me. However, her brother James refused to let us be together, and she took her own life."

"Do you regret that she died?" Izzy asked.

I considered her question. Even after so much time I didn't have a clear answer. What puzzled me more was that my heart still sank like a coin in a well at the mention of Sibyl's name. "I was grieved to hear she'd died, of course. But it was her choice to take her own life. I regret that she felt alone in the world. I regret that she felt she had no other way. I regret that I played a part in that isolation."

"Did you love her?"

I looked down at my hands again, finally feeling the shame I deserved. "No, I didn't love her. I was a young man—infatuated, in lust—but it was never love."

Izzy stood up from behind the desk and came around to lean on the edge in front of me. She was so close I could smell the soap and shampoo she'd used to wash my scent from her body only hours ago. "And what does that have to do with me?"

I scanned her face, her hair, the curve of her neck. "Because you could be her twin. And I think you're the reincarnation of her, sent here to give me another chance. Or maybe to punish me for my indulgences."

She gripped the edge of the desk and rocked forward to stare at her feet. "Is that it?"

"I think so. I don't have many secrets."

She snorted. "But the ones you do have are whoppers."

With a long sigh she stepped away from the desk and around me to open the door. "You should go. This is a lot to take in and I need to be alone to do it."

I grabbed the phone on the desk and slid it off the edge. There was nothing showing in her features and I couldn't get a clear read on whether she believed me or not. Maybe she thought I was insane now. I nodded and stepped to the opening. Before I exited, I leaned in and pressed a soft kiss to her cheek. "Just in case," I whispered.

Her fingers tightened on the door, the knuckles going white. "In case of what?"

I tried to keep the sorrow from my tone as I walked out. "In case you never let me touch you again."

I got to the street and walked home. Michael needed some rest and I needed to clear my head. I'd been alive before Izzy and I'd be alive after her. Her rejection of me would change nothing.

Except now I had to live with this pit from hell in the bottom of my gut every time I thought about her, or smelled peaches, or walked into my own flat. If she didn't believe me, she could out me to the board, try to get me kicked off the committee to make decisions for the theater. Even though I owned it, the building was a historical site and run by general committee.

I dove into the memories of Sibyl. All of which had been so fresh since I met Izzy. The last words I'd spoken to her were in anger, me pushing her away, trying to preserve her feelings. I'd failed miserably. I'd have to live with that guilt. And yet, 100 years later, it would seem I hadn't learned my lesson about women. Izzy could own me, body and soul, if she simply uttered a word.

I made it to my flat as the sun began to peek over the horizon. Standing in the entryway, I replayed the scene from the night before. I'd had her there, all to myself, and I'd blown it. A-fucking-gain.

I slapped my phone onto the shelf by the door and went to the bedroom, which was decorated in shades of white and gray that usually soothed me. Today they only rubbed against my raw nerves. The bedclothes were rumpled but I'd never gone to sleep so they were still tucked tight at the edges. I didn't bother pulling back the dove-colored linens, instead laying on top before kicking my shoes over the edge to hit the floor with a thwack.

Izzy's words played over in my head like an undeletable voicemail you dug out for a routine pity party. *Do you regret that she died?* Do you regret that she died?

Do you regret that she died?

I stared up at the white ceiling trying to block it all out, but my usual breathing techniques for staying in control failed me. Instead of continuing a futile effort I rolled to my side and curled up with my hand under the pillow.

In the sixty years I'd been under medical observation I'd learned that sleep is the body's rewind button. Anything could be fixed after a good night's sleep. A good night's sleep, a hot meal, and a shower.

But maybe those fucking scientists didn't have 150 years of bad choices rolling around in their memories.

IZZY

When Gray left I sat down at my desk and stared at the chair he'd occupied only seconds before. I stared for twenty minutes.

Everything he had told me was impossible right?

I wanted to believe him. But my rational brain was fighting me every step of the way.

I lifted a stack of paperwork and dragged my laptop out from underneath. What did I search for? Super-hot immortal billionaire? I dreaded seeing what those search results would turn up.

I opened the laptop and pulled up a search bar. With an exaggerated sigh I typed in Dorian Gray. Not a single result for my Dorian Gray, almost all of them involved Oscar Wilde. This was never going to work.

I snapped the laptop closed and shoved it back under the paperwork it had been so newly liberated from.

My phone was back at my apartment. A casualty of Gray's early morning kidnapping and brain mauling.

I plucked at the edge of Jake's shirt, not liking an idea as it began to take root. Too late, already sprouting leaves and tiny acorns.

I walked back to my apartment as the sun began to filter through the avenues. The early morning crowd shuffling about stared at me as I passed. Like they'd never seen a girl in her pajamas before. I'm sure these Paris streets had seen a lot worse than my worn-in leggings.

When I got to my door a box sat propped against the frame.

"Damn it, Gray." I whispered. "This isn't giving me space."

I snatched the box from the floor and grumbled all the way to the kitchen for a knife. The box opened smoothly with a quick slice and I stared down at a leather book.

The Picture of Dorian Gray.

I opened the cover carefully and a slip of paper fluttered to my white granite countertop.

Izzy, I marked the important parts. I'm free to talk whenever you want.

I didn't open the book to the tagged pages. Instead I sat it on the counter and went for my cell phone by the bed. One missed text from Mr. 'I can't let it go' but I ignored it and dialed the number my brother gave me when he'd left for unknown destinations eight months ago.

Once I gave the passcode I hung up and waited. Five minutes passed and I got a call back from an unregistered number.

"Hello, dear sister," his voice cut through the line.

I sagged into my bed and lay back on the mussed covers. Hearing my brother safe and sound always gave me a renewed sense of peace. Like I could breathe a little longer. During the time that passed between our talks, my lungs slowly constricted until we spoke again.

"You sound safe," I said.

He chuckled. "I am safe. What's up?"

I threaded the edge of my blanket through my fingers and let out a sigh. "I need a favor."

"Anything."

"There's this guy."

"Do you need me to kill him and make it look like an accident?"

I rolled my eyes even though he couldn't see it. "No, I don't need anyone murdered."

"Offer stands. Especially if he hurt you."

"He didn't hurt me. I just need to know more about him."

Shuffling came through the earpiece. "Ok give me the details."

"Dorian Gray."

More shuffling. "Is that a code word I'm not familiar with?"

I wished it was. "Nope. That's his name. Claims to be *that* Dorian Gray."

"Really Iz?"

"I know how it sounds, alright? Just look into it please. He claimed he was taken by a secret government agency monitoring people with weird genes like his."

"I'll send you what I find. Are you alright?"

No. "Yes, just great."

"You're not fooling anyone here."

A hot tear slid from the corner of my eye and swiped it away. "Gotta go, Jake. Time for work. Let me know what you find out. Love you."

"Love you too, Iz. Talk soon."

The phone went dead and I let my arm fall to the bed. It slid from my hand into the sheets. More tears threatened to fall but I held them back and sat up.

Shower. Clothes. Adulting for now. Wallowing later.

Once I shuffled into the bathroom I stared at myself in the mirror and decided to skip the shower. I brushed my teeth, wet and brushed my hair flat, and swiped on some mascara.

I had a troupe of actors to calm down, a billionaire on my case, and a studio director showing up at my office any minute.

I pulled on my big girl pants, threw a few necessities in my bag, and headed back to the office.

Every step through the back halls had me peering around corners for him. I was torn between wanting to see him and not wanting to see him. At lunch I grabbed a complimentary sandwich and then went back to my desk in case he was around.

But the joy of free food from my favorite shop was tempered by the cloud hanging over my head.

I figured I had two choices. Believe him or don't. My phone vibrated across my desk and I snapped it up to check the email my brother sent. All his contacts were on multiple notifications.

A .pdf attachment. I hovered my thumb on top of the icon. Did I open it now? Later? Did I open it at all? Gray had told me the truth, or at least his version of it.

I let out a sigh. Why was I stressing so much about this? He was a guy I'd had one—barely one—night with. More than that, he was my boss and someone I didn't need to be messing around with in the first place.

I inhaled and exhaled, and then scrolled up and hovered over the delete button. It took a second of fortitude but then I clicked it and dropped my phone to the desk.

I had work to do and no time for games.

Instead of spending more time on it I grabbed the stack of scripts from a drawer and headed downstairs.

It was quiet in the auditorium in a comforting way. I sat on the edge of the stage and swung my legs into the pit.

The first script was a classic and one I'd read a thousand times. Great but not appropriate immediately after *Romeo and Juliet*.

The next script didn't strike me as the right one either. None of the next five did anything for me.

I stared at the stacks of paper. It wasn't the poor scripts' fault. It was mine. I couldn't focus on them. My mind kept shifted back to Gray and his goddamn perfect face. Perfect body. Perfect everything.

It appeared my little pep talk earlier had no effect on my libido, at least.

I stacked the scripts neatly and headed straight for Gray's office. His secretary Mina sat behind her desk.

"Is he in there?"

She jolted and dropped the pen she'd been holding. "Oh yes, go ahead."

I walked into Gray's office to find him sitting behind his desk, feet propped up, a book open in his lap.

"Is that what you get paid to do?"

He glanced up and closed the book. "I didn't expect to see you so soon."

I shrugged and sat the stack of paper on the nearby shelf of books. "I didn't expect to see you so soon either."

He lifted his feet up and over the desk to stand. "Did you need something? Or have a question?"

I locked the office door and skirted the desk to stand in front of him. "Yes actually, I did need something."

His eyes lifted an increment and he buried his hands into his pockets. Waiting. Did I have the balls to take what I wanted?

When he swiped his tongue over his full bottom lip and pulled it between his teeth, my insides went molten. "You owe me."

The look he shot me was worth the moment of uncertainty. So worth the tiny dip in my belly for coming here after all. I didn't say anything else while he watched me shimmy up onto the desk and hike my black pencil skirt around my waist. Thankfully, the man could take a hint.

He locked eyes with me as he shrugged out of his jacket and laid it over the back of his chair. Then he loosed his tie and popped his collar button. My mouth watered just looking at him, knowing what all that toned skin felt like under his clothes. It was almost as good as having him naked. Almost.

He got down to his knees, gripped my lower thighs hard, and shoved my legs apart. It could have been his way of tricking himself that he was in control here. I'd let him think that if it helped.

I lifted my hips so he could get my panties off and scooted to the edge of the desk. He stared at my wet pussy like it was oxygen he needed to maintain life. A vital necessity. And when his mouth took over and he delved his lips and tongue between my legs I realized it all had very well been worth it.

His hands came around to cup my ass so I was barely situated on the desk anymore. He shoved his face into my core, all the while driving my hips forward to take more. I reached out and took the edge of the desk, holding on while he licked and sucked and fucked me with his tongue.

Oh, this was exactly what I needed. Every bit of my body ignited at the touch of his lips. My nipples pebbled hard under my blouse and I cupped one of my breasts to try and stop the ache there. But the press of his tongue was beginning a new rhythm that sent that pressure exactly against my clit. I dropped the hand from my boob and into his hair, trying to rub myself faster, harder, deeper. Then he sucked my swollen bud into his mouth and it almost shattered me. I lay back on top of his desk in hopes I could get closer, increase the pressure, anything. So close. So fucking close.

My body began to quake as my orgasm surged up, breaking in his mouth, and I let go, almost screaming, catching a hand across my mouth as he sucked my clit and shoved two fingers into my already squeezing tunnel. He fucked me like that, with his tongue, his teeth, his fingers, his whole damn face. When I started to come back to myself he eased off carefully, releasing the pressure on my clit slowly like the dial on a pressure cooker until the heat of him was gone and I was left empty and aching for more.

I opened my eyes and spots danced across his white ceiling. Other sensations filtered in like the tilt of my hips at a strange angle and the paper cut I had on my ass cheek from a stack of papers underneath me. Now that I'd gotten off, I believed I'd be able to think more rationally about the situation. But sitting up to see Gray come back with a warm wet washrag and clean me up only made me want to roll over and present my ass so he could fuck me as he should have last night.

He wiped me gently and put my panties back on. All the while I watched him carefully. Looking for a sign, maybe proof that I could see that he was telling the truth about being a 150-year-old immortal.

"You're staring at me funny."

"Where did you learn to do that?"

He ducked his head, rubbed his neck, and grinned one of those sexy playboy grins. Not the empty mask one, but the one I could feel in my toes. "A brothel in London."

I couldn't help but chuckle as his cheeks took on a telling shade of pink. "Are you blushing? How old were you?"

He shrugged. "In my thirties, I think. I wanted to know how to please a woman. Most of my life I'd been learning about my own pleasure, never how to make a woman come. I wanted that power too."

And he wielded it well. I let out a sigh and hopped off the desk. Once my skirt was back in place and I'd shoved his paperwork into a pile, I grabbed my scripts and stopped at the door. "Thank you."

"Thank you?"

I tipped my chin to the desk and walked out. If I stayed any longer I'd see what else those prostitutes had taught him.

DORIAN

My hands shook as she walked out, so I shoved them into my pockets hoping she didn't catch it. Thank you? Was that a modern adaption, to say thank you after sex like she thanked me for buying dinner or pulling out a chair?

The taste and scent of her still lingered. I would never be able to look at my desk the same way again and her response was: thank you.

I took a long breath but all that came with it was the reminder of her. I tossed the cloth I held into the sink before washing my hands and face. There was no way anything would get done after that. I adjusted the hard-on still choking in my trousers and then slipped into my jacket.

When I stepped out of the office Mina ducked her head and stared studiously at the desk. She must have heard us. Perfect. Exactly what both Izzy and I needed. I left without saying a word. Anything I could say might just embarrass us both. Instead of seeking her out I went to the corner cafe and sat outside to watch for her. I wouldn't follow her, but would ask to walk her home, so we might have a chance to talk about everything.

What did it mean? Did she believe me or did she simply want to get the end she was denied last night? I didn't mind either way but what I didn't like was not knowing where I stood, and everything between us was well into limbo at the moment.

I had no idea how long I sat there. The sun was beginning to set when some of the stage crew from the theater stopped into the cafe. I kept myself behind a newspaper. They all sat at a table nearby and chattered like hens.

I was ready to make a discreet exit when Izzy walked in. She rolled her eyes as she passed the chattering table and barely spared me a glance as I hunkered under the newspaper.

The table started up again once she went up to the counter. One girl leaned in to the other. "You know what I heard? That she's sleeping with Mr. Gray."

The blonde across the table looped herself into the conversation. "Maybe that's how you get to be producer. I'd do anything that man wanted, and he doesn't even have to give me a job."

The first girl who spoke giggled behind her coffee. "I'll give him a job."

I let out a sigh but didn't speak up. It wasn't the first time a woman had spoken about me like that, and it wouldn't be the last. What ate at me was how they spoke about Izzy. She was a damn good employee and they had no right to insinuate her job had anything to do with me.

I took a deep breath, closed the paper, and snapped it in half. The blonde who'd been facing my direction sucked in a load of air and choked, causing her friends to look back.

I met the rowdy brunette's eyes and waited for her to look away. They stayed quiet until I slipped between the tables and headed in the direction I knew Izzy would take. Hopefully the hens would go home before she came out. It took five more minutes for her to pass the doorway I'd been leaning on.

"Are you following me?" I called out.

She snorted into her coffee cup and pulled it away to wipe her lips. "Well you do have some pretty useful skills."

"Like suave good looks and an excellently alphabetized library?"

That earned me another chuckle. "Amongst other things."

"Can I walk you home?"

She ambled back and forth on the sidewalk kicking her foot. "I guess you can, as long as you know I won't invite you up."

"Of course. I just want a chance to talk a little bit."

She didn't answer but started toward her home and I fell in step beside her. The summer air was fragrant from nearby flowerbeds and the wind blew just on the good side of cool. It felt almost normal, meandering the Paris streets with her. Like we might be a couple.

But that wasn't the case, as she kept reminding me.

"Can we start over?"

She glanced at me then back down the road. "Why do we need to start over? I didn't think we needed a redo. I actually thought I was very clear about what this is or isn't."

My hands began to shake again and I put them in my pockets. "Yes, you were clear about what you wanted. But I'm a businessman and an excellent negotiator. And I want you."

She jerked to a stop. "Say that again."

"I want you."

She took another swig of coffee and gave me a long look. One of those weighed and measured sort of looks that leave you feeling naked.

"I would like to say yes but I really don't think that's a good idea."

I swallowed the lump growing wider and wider in my throat. "Is it because I'm your employer?"

"That, and the whole immortal thing is a little much."

This was one of the main reasons so few people knew about it. Relationships were definitely not improved by the knowledge.

And not exactly telling the truth had never been an option for me. I couldn't pretend to want to spend forever with a woman when I knew it wasn't going to be possible. I'd also never had the courage to attempt a family with my disability.

I let the disappointment roll through me. Let it sink in. That would help me get over this, I told myself. I'd latched onto Izzy giving me a chance and allowing me to right the wrongs of my past. To make up for Sibyl's death. When I first saw her it had never occurred to me that she wouldn't want me too.

"What's going on in that head of yours?"

I realized we'd been standing silently for several minutes. "Nothing. Let me walk you home and I'll be on my way."

Her eyebrows drew together into a cute little crease right above the beautiful slope of her nose. I tried to memorize everything about her in case I couldn't get this close again.

She shook her head and started walking. We went silent and my palms began to sweat more the closer we got to her door. As if that threshold would be the end for good.

"Does it scare you?"

Her question slapped me against the face but it was one I'd considered before, so I had the answer to dig out of my head. "Yes and no. I'm afraid of the life I don't get to live because of it. I won't allow myself to have children. I can't..." I gestured at her. "Have real relationships. I'm basically waiting forever to die. In that sense it doesn't scare me."

She didn't respond for a while. "And the evolution of the human race over the last 150 years, did that scare you?"

I considered that bigger question. "A lot of things have changed and a lot of things haven't. There is still so much hate in the world, so much inequality. I do enjoy the internet though. And airplanes."

"Airplanes are definitely a bonus. How did you travel around before?"

I had to think way back. "Horses, boats, that sort of thing."

"Sounds inconvenient."

"No more inconvenient than now. You still had to plan, buy tickets, pack, and leave. It just took longer to get everywhere."

We wandered silently some more until I caught sight of her door closing in on us.

"I'm sorry about this afternoon," she said, breaking the silence before we reached her building."

We stopped and I met her eyes. "You have absolutely nothing to apologize for."

"Then why do I feel guilty?"

"I don't know. You shouldn't. You didn't take anything I didn't offer gladly." I lowered my voice. "And would offer again should you wish."

Her lips curled into a smile. "Maybe in another life, Gray, we can figure this whole thing out."

I nodded and stepped closer, closing in to wrap my hands around her small waist. She met my eyes with a question but didn't say anything.

"If this is the last of you I'm going to get, then I want you to remember it."

I leaned down and brushed my lips against hers, softly and slowly. Then I ran my hands up the curve of her body to cup her cheeks and draw her into me. It took a second, but then I felt her entire body shudder in my hands and she let go, pressing into the kiss and leaving a nibble on my bottom lip. When I opened my eyes again we were both panting.

"Thank you," I whispered. Echoing her words from earlier. Her cheeks, already flushed, went a deeper red before she turned from the cradle of my arms and entered her building.

I stayed until she was out of sight. This wasn't the last time I'd see her, but if I cared about her I'd keep my distance. Her career meant a lot to her. I would protect it, and in doing so would protect her as well.

I walked home instead of calling Michael, trying to clear my head.

When I got inside I felt that familiar indifference rising up in my chest threatening to choke me. I'd been content with it for so long, now that I'd felt the pure honey of hope and longing for the first time in years, I didn't know if I could go back to that box. That tiny box where the world couldn't get in.

I stood in the middle of my living room and stared at the books. Now they only reminded me of what I didn't have.

A flash of something struck me. An incendiary grenade to the rib cage. I swept my hand along the first shelf I could reach and dragged the books to the floor. Beautiful antiques and first editions, and I didn't care. I didn't want to look at them anymore.

It was as if losing Sibyl a second time had shown me I wasn't meant to live in this world.

I should have died years ago. Decades ago.

Maybe it was time to figure out how.

IZZY

When I got inside I stripped to my underwear and climbed into bed. The soft comforter and sheets cocooned me in silence and I felt like I could breathe for the first time all day—the first time in the last few days, even.

The first thought that came to my head was Gray. Maybe I'd been too hard on him. Or maybe I hadn't given him a proper chance.

The other part of my brain told me to lock it up, that he and I had only been seeing each other for a few days. I shouldn't feel like I owed him anything. I didn't.

And yet, this guilt ate at me from the inside, turning my belly and the coffee I'd drunk into a rolling drum on the back of a concrete truck.

The longing for home hit me hard. For the first time since I'd arrived to work in Paris, all I wanted to do was crawl into bed in my own apartment in New York. I wanted the Chinese food smells to drift into my window and to get too drunk too early at Sunday brunch. I wanted Jake. Damn, I wanted Jake to wrap me up in his big arms and let him tell me everything would be all right, even if we both knew it was a lie.

We were good at that, lying to save each other.

I don't know how long I stayed that way, curled up in my blankets longing for my brother like a little girl. It was dark before the growl in my stomach forced me out of bed to the kitchen.

I poured some corn flakes in a bowl and doused them with milk and a couple teaspoons of sugar before hiking myself up onto the cold granite to eat.

I'd forgotten I sat my phone there and when I opened the screen I found a missed call from an unknown number and two text messages.

I opened the text:

Excuse me for texting you, Miss. This is Michael, Mr. Gray's driver. Can you come to his flat immediately? I'm downstairs now and can take you as soon as you are ready.

Crap. I checked the time. He'd only sent it ten minutes ago. I went to the window and sure enough, he was at the curb.

If Gray thought he could summon me like some sort of...well, whatever, he had another thing coming.

I sat the bowl in the sink and padded to my room to get dressed. Another soft pair of leggings and my favorite Captain America T-shirt this time. I grabbed my keys and phone and went to meet Michael.

Once I got outside he rushed to open the door. "Getting faster Michael, but for the record I'm only going so I can tell him off in person."

"Tell him off?"

"If he thinks he can just summon me, he'll soon learn something about my fist."

"He didn't summon you, Miss. I'm the one who texted you. He didn't ask for you."

I stopped as I began to climb in the car and braced my hand on the doorframe. "What? Why? Start talking, Mikey."

"You'll see when we get there."

He gently pushed the door to urge me inside and closed it behind me. In record time we made it to Gray's building and Michael escorted me all the way to his door.

Memories of the last time I'd been here started to filter in but I pushed past them and went inside.

The apartment was dark, Michael stayed in the hall as I closed the door behind me. The only light came in from the street through the windows, and even then we were mostly too high up for it.

I felt along the wall for a light switch and flipped it as soon as my hand brushed its ridged surface.

The room washed in light, and it took my eyes a minute to process. The perfect living room was now trashed, a pile of books spread across the gorgeous hardwood. Gray lay on his back on the couch in nothing but boxer briefs and black socks.

"Gray?"

He didn't stir at the sound of my voice. I walked over, carefully tiptoeing past books that likely cost more than my car at home. Wonder what kind of insurance he had to carry.

"Gray," I called again.

Still nothing.

I looked down at his face, his eyes closed, his hair still somehow perfect. There was a smear of blood on his knuckles and I grabbed them to examine but no cut marred his perfect skin.

Creepy.

"Gray," I said and shook his shoulder.

He gasped and opened his eyes, causing me to jump back and trip over a pile of books only to land on my ass into another pile.

Oh this was going to be painful tomorrow.

He sat up and rubbed his eyes. "Why is it so bright?"

I huffed. Angrier now than before. "I turned on the light, obviously."

He blinked and met my eyes. Something was off about him. Like his mind played a song on repeat but in the wrong tune. Instead of sounding unique it just sounded haunting.

"What are you doing here?" he asked, leaning over to brace his elbows on his thighs.

I extricated myself from the pile of books and glared. "I'm asking myself that question right now too. Michael texted me and asked me to get over here."

His tone took an edge. "You're here for Michael?"

I sat gingerly beside him, my ass and back aching from the book landing. "No, dumbass, I'm here because he was worried about you."

I gestured at the books. "For obvious reasons. What's the problem?"

He sucked in a long breath and sat back. That perfectly impenetrable playboy billionaire mask in place. The one I thought he'd gotten rid of with me. The one that sort of stung to look at after everything that had happened between us.

"I'm sorry you concerned yourself. You didn't need to come."

I looked around at the books, his pile of clothing nearby. Obviously something was wrong with him. Maybe this was the slowly losing his mind bit he mentioned.

"Well, you're lying." I tried to think of what Jake would do in this situation. "Have you eaten?"

He blinked at me like I'd asked him if he had an extra hand somewhere it didn't belong. His stomach let out a loud rumble but his face stayed the same. It was sort of eerie, actually.

I slipped off the couch and tiptoed into the kitchen. It looked like the rest of his house. Stainless steel, beautiful granite, luxurious hardwood. Rich sophistication. I opened the refrigerator to find five items: cheese, wine, heavy cream, mayonnaise, and butter.

Either he didn't grocery shop or he didn't eat. Was that an immortal thing?

I shook the thought away. Of course not, he wasn't a vampire.

His pantry proved a little more fruitful and I grabbed a box of pasta and began water boiling. While he was in the other room I opened another drawer out of curiosity. Cutlery, tea bags, wine bottle opener. His kitchen reminded me of a stage kitchen. Only the props necessary to make it appear to be real.

"Dorian, do you ever eat in here?" I called out to him.

A few seconds passed and he came in rubbing the back of his neck. It was both sexy as hell and disconcerting, witnessing him walking around in his underwear.

"Pardon?"

I pointed to the drawers. "You have nothing in your kitchen. Do you ever eat here?"

He looked at his own kitchen like he'd never seen it before. "No, rarely. I usually order out or I have Michael bring me food."

Ah the joys of money. Must be nice.

"Well, tonight you are going to enjoy the culinary stylings of me. The vast majority of these revolve around microwaving, boiling water, and pouring cereal."

The corner of his lip twitched for a second but then his mask was back in place. "I really appreciate the effort you are going to on my part. I'll eat and then you can get out of here. I'm sure you have plans."

I hopped up on the counter and turned to face him cross-legged. He eyed me but said nothing.

"I don't have anything planned. And Dorian, I didn't say we couldn't be friends. I just don't think it's a good idea to date."

He hung his head for a second and then lifted it. "I'd like that."

To be fair, as he sat there almost completely naked my feelings weren't entirely platonic. Those V cuts at his hips I'd only gotten to hold onto the other night were really distracting.

"Um, since we are being friendly. Do you think you could put some pants on?"

He didn't respond but got up and went into his bedroom. Part of me wanted to see it but I also knew there was a very real chance I wouldn't want to leave once I got a good look. At him and the bed.

He returned a few minutes later and I put the noodles into the boiling pot.

"I'm surprised you didn't have plans tonight," he offered by way of awkward conversation. I'd figured we were way past weekend plans and the weather but I humored him.

"I'm more of a homebody. I'll go for a beer every now and again but mostly I stay in waiting for my brother to call."

Something passed across his features, shifting, and he truly met my eyes for the first time since I arrived. "You have a brother?"

"Yes, his name is Jake."

He leaned across the counter and chuckled. "Do you believe in fate?"

"Not something I'd ever really thought about before, why?"

He instantly sobered. "Sibyl had a brother too. His name was James."

That was a weird coincidence. I believed what he said, but I wasn't sure I believed the whole past life thing.

"Is he older than you?"

"A little bit older."

He nodded. The water was beginning to boil harder so I stirred the noodles and fished one out to taste. Perfect.

I drained them and mixed them with butter and the Parmesan he'd had in his refrigerator. When I put the plate on the bar for him he stared at it curiously.

"It's not going to bite you. And I used your groceries, so if they aren't good that's on you, not me."

"No, I'm sure they are fine." He took a bite and then another. I watched a minute as he ate the pasta very fast, barely pausing to draw breath. Once he finished I was only halfway through my own and he looked up.

"There's more if you're still hungry."

He let out a sigh. "No, that was delicious. Do you want some wine?"

"Sure, what do you have?"

He left the room and my curiosity outweighed the need to keep eating. I followed to a cedar-lined room with rows upon rows of wine bottles lying sideways in X shaped boxes. "Wow. That is a lot wine."

"I do enjoy wine. Living in France affords me a unique opportunity to acquire amazing bottles."

I ran my fingertips along the bottle tops. Not a speck of dust coated their surfaces.

He plucked a bottle and held it up. "Do you like red?"

I laughed. "I like wine."

"Fair enough." We went back to the kitchen and he opened the bottle to pour it into a glass pitcher. "Give it a second," he said before spinning to locate a couple wine glasses.

I took my seat on the counter again and dove back into my food. At least he looked better, a little more himself, despite the mask still being very much in place.

I couldn't decide why that was bothering me so much. That he felt he had to hide from me, especially since I knew his secrets, at least the one I hoped was his biggest.

He poured a glass and handed it to me.

"This is fancy," I commented. "I usually drink my wine from the bottle.

His face. He clutched his metaphorical pearls and waited for me to take a sip. It was deep, dry, and coated my tongue in a beautiful array of dark chocolate and strawberry.

"Oh man, that is good. I took another small sip and sat it on the counter next to me. "Definitely not something I could drink from a bottle."

He took his own stool again and sipped from his glass. "I'd hope not. We would have to discontinue this friendship if you tried."

I chuckled and ate some more. "Well, now I know how to get rid of you."

It had been a joke but it hit something in him, his smile drooped and he stared into his glass. Shit. Opening my mouth was becoming dangerous these days.

"I didn't think about what I was saying. I'm sorry."

He waved it away, mask firmly back in place. "Don't worry about it. You shouldn't feel you have to censor yourself." He stood. "Thank you for the meal. I'm going to go start on that mess."

I wanted to ask what had happened there but he probably would lie, make up something to maintain his ordered calm.

Damn it, why did I care so much? What was it about him that made me want to ruffle every part of his perfectly ordered life?"

I shoved a few more bites of noodles in my mouth and then slid off the counter.

He was sitting, cradling a stack of books in his hands when I went back into his living room.

When he looked up there was no mask.

His handsome features were empty, save his eyes, which begged for something I didn't quite understand.

DORIAN

She couldn't see me like this. I turned away and took a long inhale to press all the crazy spiraling in my brain down into a manageable pocket. A rejection, so what? People dealt with it every day. I could too. Except my mind wouldn't just let it go, inserting whispers like: do other people have so much sin to carry around? Do other people have death on their hands like you do?

I focused on quieting all thought and instead stacking books. They were mostly out of order, with a few exceptions of little groupings that had stuck together in the fall. The leather-bound covers protected most of the pages.

Poor sad Hemingway lay open with bent pages at the corner of the rug. I shifted across the pile to grab the book but Sibyl beat me to it.

No. Not Sibyl. Izzy.

She handed it over, twisted her legs underneath her to sit, and began to stack books. I was thankful for the silence; not so much the long lingering concerned looks. We worked quietly and I avoided glancing her way. The memories of that long lithe body in my arms were too fresh, not to mention the red stain coating my hands every time I glanced down at them for longer than a minute.

Holy hell, it was happening. The doctors told me I wouldn't be able to last two hundred years. That my mental stamina would deteriorate. Maybe Izzy had been the trigger, releasing the guilt I felt about Sibyl, and now it became an avalanche soon to take out everything in its path.

I looked up at Izzy who froze in the act of stacking two corresponding volumes together. "What? Why are you looking at me like that?"

I usually had more control over my emotions and whatever the rest of the world got to see of them. I closed my eyes and forced the thoughts away, somewhere, anywhere, so Izzy couldn't read them in my eyes.

I shuffled the piles I'd stacked forward, putting them back onto the shelf, and then surged to my feet and went to the bedroom. The slammed door behind me should keep her out, I hoped. I could hide like a coward until she left, right?

"Dorian?" She called through the door and her voice was enough to have me reaching for the handle. I stopped. No. She had to stay out, get away, before I became unsafe, unstable, unhinged.

"Dorian? You can talk to me. What happened out here?"

I grasped for any excuse I could think of before pushing myself to the corner and shouting across the room. "Nothing, I'm fine. I think maybe that butter went bad."

The soft scrape of her fingers sliding down the door echoed into the quiet. I prayed she'd leave, go back to her apartment, and forget about me. She'd made it clear she didn't want me, so it should be easy for her to walk away.

Dr. Robertson was the only person who could help me now. The last time I'd been at the science center they'd told me when the end came they could put me to sleep and stop my vital organs; very much like a prison execution but without the pain. Was that my only choice? Death by lethal injection, after 150 years on this planet? After everything I'd seen and done and been through? It almost seemed like cowardice, cheating the punishment and karma I deserved for the atrocities I'd committed in my younger years. For the people I'd hurt. I couldn't bear it if Izzy became one of them.

There was silence at the door and for a moment I thought she'd left. Then I caught a thump against the bottom of the frame. Her shadow stretched underneath and I could see the edge of her T-shirt under the door. She was sitting in front of it now. I cleared my throat quietly. "You should go home. I'll be alright."

Another thump and then a curse. "No, I'll wait, make sure you're ok. You might need something."

I lay my head down on my arms as they crossed over my knees. Was this woman's will forged in iron? I racked my brain for another way to get rid of her. Only one came to mind and it would hurt us both. Could I cause her even a little pain to protect her from the looming avalanche that could engulf her?

Yes.

I let out a long sigh and climbed to my feet. It took five minutes to dress, my best suit and tie. Then I shaved and combed my hair. When I'd finished and looked in the mirror I appeared the same perfect specimen I always presented. Nothing of the fracture in my mind was visible, at least to me. I even bolstered myself with a smile, one I'd known to be cold and unyielding. The hard part would be getting out the door without looking at her too long. If I stayed and met her eyes, then I might very well break.

Was I strong enough for this? Not at all. I could already feel the micro-fissures under the mask beginning to spread. I didn't have very long to escape.

I sat on the edge of my bed, slipped on my shoes, and set my cufflinks. Then I shook my shoulders and stepped to the door. I opened it carefully at first so she didn't fall over, but then fast, as if I were jerking it once I could see she sat up straight on the floor.

She looked up the long line of my body from her cross-legged position on the hardwood. "Going somewhere?"

I didn't meet her eyes but stalked around for my phone, which I found on the shelf by the door. I texted Michael for the car and stayed turned away from her before I answered. "Yes, I'm feeling much better and I think it's a good night to hit the town. I have a friend who is meeting me."

"A friend?" she asked. I locked onto how I'd felt when she told me she didn't want me, let it sink in and strengthen my spine before I turned back.

She stood with her arms crossed under her breasts, head tilted to the side, nothing but questions in her eyes.

I threw her that cold, calculating smile I'd perfected for business meetings and people I wanted out of my presence. "Well, she's a little more than a friend."

Izzy flinched like I'd struck her. I tightened my hand on the doorknob, using it as a grounding point. "Thank you for coming over. I'll get the help to put the books back. It was merely an accident. Do you want me to walk you out? I'd invite you to stay but I'll likely be coming back here with company."

Her mouth dropped open before she shook herself and stalked forward. All five-foot-eight inches of her drawn up in anger stirred me in a way it shouldn't have. She was marvelous to behold. I knew she held back a biting tirade and I wanted it. I deserved it. I needed it to keep pushing her away.

She put her finger inches from my face, her lips twisted in fury. Then she stopped and dropped her hand. I fell with it. I needed that anger to get her out of here. When I opened my mouth to try another verbal disassociation tactic, she slapped me across the face, hard and fast. My head snapped to the side and when I looked back at her she held her hand in the other.

I wanted to comfort her, get ice for her, do anything to get that look of betrayal off her face. Instead, I touched my lip where it stung the most. No blood. Then I crooked my chin. "You should put some ice on that."

She narrowed her eyes and slapped me again. "Stop it." She growled. "I'm not a damn idiot. I know what you're trying to do and if I have to, I'm going to keep slapping you until I knock some sense into that ancient brain of yours."

I grabbed the door handle once more. If I left she'd have no reason to stay. I could hide in the car and come back after she went home. She clutched my forearm hard and raised a questioning brow. "I'm not playing games with you, Gray. You seem to be good at them, but I will tip the board over every single time."

I swallowed, using everything I had left to maintain a neutral expression. Using the sting in my cheeks to lock eyes with her. "You're welcome to join us. Me and Yvette. She doesn't mind company."

Another slap. I took in a shuddering breath. "Do not hit me again."

"What are you going to do? Hit me back? I'd like to see you try it."

I released the door and stepped forward, real anger started to merge with the fake until I couldn't find the line between. "I would never hit a woman."

"Oh yeah, did you hit any in the past? Should I go check that book so I can find out?"

The mention of the book pushed it too far; I think we both realized it at the same time. I surged forward to trap her body between mine and the wall beside the door. Inches away from her face I spit out. "You will not hit me again."

We both stayed caught-in-the-act still, breathing heavily. My hands clasped her waist, hers in fists pressed against my chest. It was a classic angry couple movie scene, except in my living room. How did I let it get this far? Sense began to filter in and I started to pull my hands from her waist.

She must have felt the shift in pressure because her fists uncurled to lock around my jacket lapels and keep me there. "We aren't through here."

"No, I'm entirely sure we are through. You've made it clear on multiple occasions you don't want me. And yet when I ask you to leave, you resist and find excuses. So who is playing games here, Izzy?"

Her eyes widened a little and some of the anger left them. She swallowed heavily, still clutching my jacket.

What did I do now? Wait until it fizzled and she let me go? I didn't think that was possible as the solid warm press of her body, along with the sparks zipping through me from my residual fury, stirred something else in me.

Her eyes widened further as her realization of the source of my own expression sunk in. She'd understand fully in a few seconds. I gripped her small hands in mine, still locked in my jacket.

"Isobel."

She sagged and fluttered her eyes closed as I said her full name.

"If you do not release me at once, this is going to go very badly. Probably for both of us."

"Wh-what are you going to do?" Her voice was soft, fluttering, oh so sweet. It wasn't a question she really wanted an answer to.

I drew in a long breath, intending to let her go and walk out. *Gray…just let her go and walk out.*

Let her go and walk out.

I released her fingers slowly and she sagged back against the wall. The second I took my eyes off hers she lunged forward and slapped me again. Harder than before.

There was no anger in her eyes now. All I saw was invitation.

IZZY

My heart beat so loudly in my chest I was sure he could hear the echoing thump thump thump against my ribcage.

Did he know what I was asking? Did I know what I was asking? Before I could let the potential fear kick in, I gave my mind over to my body, and lifted my arm to slap him one more time.

He grabbed my wrist in a crushing grip, stalling its progress before I could strike him.

There was no give in that look. Not one. Single. Inch. For the first time, I met his eyes and saw something to fear, but I didn't fear for myself. That look said he'd been to the brink of insanity and stood just on the good side. One push might send him over. So I swallowed my hurt pride, let him squeeze my wrist a little too tight, and popped up onto my tiptoes to finally taste sin.

But he wouldn't let me reach his lips. His other hand closed around my throat, not squeezing, but cradling it. I knew he understood exactly what I wanted right now, what I needed right now, and I let him take control.

He spun me to face the wall. His body aligned behind mine and he released me to rip open the bottom of my shirt. I mourned Cap for a brief second. The rough handling and the loose hold sent the fabric scraps to my ankles. I swallowed the knifepoint of fear threatening to slice open the moment and bleed it dead. No. He wanted me and I wanted him. I didn't expect it like this but I was in no way unwilling. My pants were next as he roughly shoved them to my feet along with my panties.

"Put your hands on the wall and don't move," he said in my ear. More growl than an actual directive.

I spread my arms out and anchored my fingertips in the brick, the scratchy grooves between the rectangles giving me something to anchor to. It should have felt like a police frisking. Cold and unmovable, with my bare ass out and him completely clothed behind me.

The heat of his body through his clothes warmed me, excited me, aroused me in a way I didn't know was possible.

I cleared my throat to speak, but he clamped a hand over my mouth.

"Don't. If you want to stop, you have to explicitly say stop. No matter what happens or how many rounds you think we've gone. Do you understand? When you say stop I will let you go completely." He released his hold over my mouth and buried his face into the back of my hair. "Tell me to stop. Tell me to stop now," he begged.

My body reacted before my mind and reached around to hold the back of his neck. I wasn't going to say stop. He'd started this and now he was going to have to see it through.

"Put your hand back on the wall," he snapped after as second of us standing, breathing, beating together.

The fear left me. He was in control and some dark twisted part of me liked it that way. To surrender to him. To give up that gnawing part of my always questioning mind.

At the same time, it wasn't always like this. We had been in a reverse position only hours before and both of us wrangled for control then too. It seemed this time he'd won. Next time I would.

His hands traced the curves of my bare hips, and I caught a whisper in a foreign language I didn't recognize. Right now I couldn't ask what it meant, but I filed away the information for later.

He slid those long fingers over the curves of my thighs to my core, only inches from touching the part of me that ached for it. "Do you know what I'm going to do to you?"

He didn't want an answer, so I stayed silent, cheek pressed against the wall. Instead of reaching between my thighs, he released me all together but kept his lips near my ear, the only bit of him touching me now. "Go to my bed. Ass in the air. Do it now."

I scuttled with my pants around my ankles and paused long enough to untangle them and toss them away. I pushed open his bedroom door and went straight to the bed. Once my hips were centered over my ankles I risked a glance back at him. Something had softened in his face. No. I didn't want that. He needed this release and so did I.

When I shifted to move off the bed, the hard edges returned to his gaze. "Don't you dare fucking move."

I froze and put my knee back in place, but it was too late. He stalked across the room and struck my bare ass with his open palm in one hard thwack. The pain bloomed slowly as the sharp initial sting released. That bloom heated me thoroughly. He put a hand on either hip. I wanted to look back, see his face, but I kept my head forward.

"Izzy," he whispered.

I rolled over, and tucked my hips under to land on my ass. His eyes glistened softly. "I can't give you what you want."

Not a fucking option. I scooted and bounced myself off the bed until I stood chest to chest with him. "Do we need to run through this again?"

He blinked and I squared my shoulders and slapped his face again. His jaw clenched and his lips tightened but he didn't move, or say anything.

I reached out to do it again but he grabbed my wrist, hard, like I wanted it.

Before I knew it, he'd spun me around, shoved my face in the coverlet, and pushed inside me hard and fast. I was wet, and thought I was ready for that invasion, but nothing could have prepared me.

He held my upper back, pressing me into the bed, and fucked me with what I could only assume was decades of pent-up anger and frustration.

Each shove of his hard length inside me was accompanied by a hard exhale, and the sound made me more wet for him. I could only keep my mouth and nose free to breathe and hang on to the bedding as he pounded into me. He took up a harder rhythm and moved the hand that had been holding my back up to join the other to clutch my hips.

I took a gasping breath as now he had the leverage to yank me back into him until the entire length of his cock was stuffed inside me. Then he stopped.

I exhaled, shaking, and then stilled and waited. What would he do next? I'd told him no anal but right now I might have even negotiated that. Not to mention the fact that he was fucking me bareback and we hadn't even had that conversation. It felt illicit and sensual.

He flexed his fingers around my hips, digging them in one by one so they curled up to my hipbones. I jerked back as he slid one of them forward between my legs and passed his index finger over my aching neglected clit.

"You feel so good," he whispered, drawing me toward him now, moving in and out of me slowly with the time of his fingers playing music on my body.

It was as if the rage was gone and the gentleman Dorian returned. I risked a glance around to see his eyes focused on where his cock slid in and out of me. No indifference there at least. The look was something I hadn't seen on his face before. Even when he'd pounded into my face in his entryway. This was reverence and worship and the fucking way to my heart.

I turned back to focus on the bedding. His dick pulling me apart, his fingers rubbing me closer and closer to orgasm. I focused so hard it began began to slip away. He must have noticed the shift in me because he removed his hand at my core and placed it back on my hips. Another second passed and he carefully slipped from my body, flipped my hips to the side, and then dragged me toward him. I loved a man who knew how to handle a woman's body.

He opened my legs, climbed between them, and was inside me again. The weight of him on my belly and chest, and the ability to look into his eyes, made the act deeper, more meaningful. The exact opposite of what I was going for.

The bastard caught that too and leaned down to kiss me. Hard and fast, gone in seconds, but the press of his lips lingered. I opened my eyes and let out a sigh. "Get off."

He blinked but continued his slow and steady entry and retreat into my body. As if he had it timed on some internal clock.

"I'm not feeling this anymore, get off."

The corner of his lip quirked up and a prick of fear shot through me along with a wave of adrenaline and splash of curiosity-laced arousal. He raised an eyebrow, daring me to push him away.

I tried, pushing his chest but he didn't move. "I told you to get off,"

I said with no real heat, my pussy already flooded with new interest.

He said nothing, did nothing but stared into my eyes. I opened my mouth to repeat myself, knowing he wouldn't do anything, not caring either way, and then he smashed his hand across my lips, the edge of his palm under my nose leaving barely enough room to breathe. And between seconds my entire body lit with fire like I'd never known. Every inch of my skin woke up and tuned to the way he slowly rocked his hips forward, the scent of his hand that smelled like my arousal, and the way his eyes darkened above me.

Fuck, Gray.

He picked up the pace and I gasped and moaned and writhed under his hand. He dragged his own lip between his teeth as I darted my tongue out, licking the inside of his fingers while I stared into his eyes. After a minute his pace took an unsteady rhythm and the knowledge he was close to coming ratcheted my looming orgasm even higher. He let go of my mouth and braced his hands on either side of me now, arching his back so his face remained close to stare into my eyes.

"Do you want to stop?" he asked. It wasn't a real question. The wet heat gripping him tight was enough for him to know that.

"If you stop now I might just figure out a way to kill you, Gray."

He smiled. A new smile. One I hadn't seen before. With teeth and those damnable full lips, and its sexiness practically punched me in the gut.

"Are you close?" he asked, his breathing going erratic now.

"Yes," I managed, reaching around to hold on to his ribs, digging my nails in as he surged faster and harder into me.

One second I hovered at the edge of it and then I fell in. Like walking off a safe stable ship deck into a roiling ocean. I held onto Gray through the storm. He collapsed on top of me, all his weight wrapped in my arms as he surged inside me again and again and again. Then finally he stopped, his entire body quaking with an unsteady exhale.

The silence in the room was unsettling after the noise of our lovemaking. I blinked back to reality, releasing my hold on him. He didn't move and I couldn't help but chuckle as he laid there, his sweaty forehead tucked against the side of my neck. I almost drifted to sleep when a sharp pain on my shoulder ripped me out of it.

"What the hell?" I yelled andopened my eyes to glare.

He smiled, that damn fucking real smile I didn't even know he had. The one that loosened the reigns on my doubt about him. The one I sort of wished I'd never even seen. "That's for earlier," he whispered before rolling his weight off me and pulling me in tight to curl up in front of him.

I let out a long steady exhale allowing him to cocoon me with his body. "I think I hate you a little, Dorian Gray."

He kissed the back of my shoulder and whispered, "good. It's probably better that way."

DORIAN

I woke some time in the middle of the night, the sweat and effects of our lovemaking dry on my skin and hers. She stirred and then curled up in the covers. It was peaceful watching her like that.

I went to the bathroom to get a washcloth and cleaned her up the best I could without waking her. She moaned when I touched her thighs and the trust she put in me hit me all over. When she'd started trying to fight with me I knew exactly where she would take it, and so many times I'd wanted to stop it. How I had treated her…

A bruise was starting to form on the curve of her neck and I could clearly make out a couple bruises on the soft fleshy parts of her hips in the bathroom light. Damn, I was careless.

I took a quick shower and went into the living room. The clock on the stove rolled over to 5:00 just as I started water for tea. Going back to bed was what I truly wanted but I didn't trust myself to be around her. As the water boiled I pulled out a notepad and pen from a drawer by the door. As quickly as possible I scribbled out my feelings to her, and why I thought it best we stay away from each other from now on. Once I finished I tapped the pad's edge on the counter, considering.

Would it be easier to just leave? If I weren't in France, then surely the temptation wouldn't be present for either of us. I pulled the kettle off the stove and peeked into the bedroom to make sure it hadn't woken her. A snore answered as I peered through the dark. An ache started in my chest and I wasn't entirely sure I could give her up. It wouldn't be the first selfish thing I did in my life, and likely not the last.

My conscience had grown pretty adept at right and wrong after so many years, but I had no idea what to do here. She'd told me repeatedly she didn't want to be with me, and yet she kept coming back. I knew without a doubt that what had happened between us last night was what we'd both wanted. What we'd both needed.

Did she wrestle with staying or going too? Were her attempts to push me away the same as the ones I'd tried on her?

The thought curled up in my head, casting doubt on the last few days we'd spent together. Was it wrong to stay with her?

Yes.

After the incident with the books and seeing Sibyl's face whenever I was with Izzy. Yes. Nothing good could come of a relationship between us if I was going mad. The doctors warned me it would happen every single year for the last almost fifty. I didn't expect it to happen so soon. Well, I supposed soon was a relative term in this situation.

I quickly made a cup of tea and prayed the cream in the refrigerator was still good. Smelled all right. I sat at the counter to drink my tea, eyeing the pad and pen sitting at the end. Was it enough? Could it push her away?

I thought so, but I'd thought the little act I'd pulled last night would push her away too. In either case she'd be hurt. And now, after we'd slept together, it would hurt her more. Damn it, there was no way to win this.

I sipped the tea, trying with every ounce of brainpower she hadn't completely mummified last night to decide. The echo of her fingers still played across my skin. Every breath, every moan, every response of her body to mine. I'd remember it forever.

Sibyl and I had a very short time together. And nothing as far into abandon as what Izzy gave me. The more time I spent with her the more

I realized she was nothing at all like Sibyl, aside from her appearance.

A light knock came at the front door. I glanced at the clock: 5:30. Who would be here at this hour? My only thought was Michael but he usually took off at 3:00 am and I didn't see him again until lunchtime the next day unless I texted to wake him—something I tried not to do as I ran the man ragged on regular days. He didn't need to deal with me any more than necessary on his time off.

I grabbed my pants off the floor and slipped them on. If it was Michael it didn't matter if he saw my underwear. If it was someone else, well, they shouldn't be visiting so early.

I opened the door and a man stood there, back to me, brown leather jacket, jeans, a hat, black sneakers. He turned after a second and something clicked in my head. He looked so familiar, but I couldn't place him.

"Are you Dorian Gray," he asked. American accent. Interesting.

I nodded. "Can I help you?"

He peered into my flat, his eyes seeming to miss nothing, including the pile of clothes on the floor and Izzy's ripped comic book T-shirt.

The man held out his hand. "It's nice to finally meet you. I'm Jake."

Unable to do much else, I shook his hand. "Pleasure is all mine. Do I know you?"

He smiled, a deep dimple in each of his bearded cheeks. His hair was a sort of auburn brown and those eyes, where had I seen those eyes before?

He released my hand and swung his arms behind his back. "No, you don't know me. I wonder if I might have a word with you about my sister, Isobel."

My two worlds converged. Izzy and Jake. Sybil and James. Except this time, I didn't intend to leave any casualties in my wake. I glanced back to make sure I'd pulled the bedroom door closed behind me. "Of course, please come in."

He stepped inside and surveyed more of what he could see. The mess on the floor, the remnants of our dinner last night on the counter. My tea steaming away on at the bar. "I'm sorry to interrupt your morning but I won't be in town long and thought I'd take the opportunity to drop by. Izzy mentioned you."

I tried to keep my eyes on the bedroom door, he took that in too. "Izzy did mention you, but she never told me what you do."

He nodded, still standing with his arms behind his back. "Oh, I'm in the Navy."

"Not much naval activity here, Mr. Vale."

He shook his head, that dimple popping out again. This man was almost as good as me at shifting emotions around his face so no one would catch them.

There was no other reason for her brother to be here than to warn me away. He was a couple inches taller than me, his shoulders wide and full. In sheer strength, the man could probably crush me.

I gestured to the couch and tried not to think about his sister's bare ass having been there only a couple nights ago. "Would you like to sit down?"

He nodded and took a seat on the very far edge of the couch, closest to the door. A wary fellow, or maybe he needed a quick escape route.

He settled and shifted his hands to his lap, knees facing me. I didn't bother worrying about my state of undress. I could have been wearing my best suit and it wouldn't change his opinion of me.

"So, was there something I could help you with, Mr. Vale?"

He nodded and rubbed his hands up and down his jeans like his palms were sweaty. And yet nothing else about him spoke of nerves. I enjoyed the way he cast doubt on what I thought he might be feeling. Making me unsteady and unsure. An interesting tactic.

"Yes, actually. I want to know what your intentions are with my sister."

Finally, we'd come to it. "Izzy is a wonderful woman. I hope to spend more time with her. At present she seems uncertain if she wants to spend more time with me."

He tilted his head to the side, and that same weighed and measured look Izzy gave me fell across his features. Oddly disconcerting, given the present situation.

"And if she tells you she doesn't want to see you again?"

I shrugged and wished I had my tea so I would at least be able to fiddle with something, look away from his scrutiny. "Then of course I'll respect her wishes. I would never purposefully harm her."

The note on the counter made that statement more than a lie. I'd definitely hurt her when I left. But causing her pain to protect her, I hoped, was a different kind of sin.

He gave me a nod that included the tilt of his shoulders. Something I'd witnessed countless times in good ol' American boys. He was trying to make me feel safe. In doing so, he was making me even more nervous.

"Was that all you wanted, Mr. Vale?"

He waved at me with a smile. "Please, call me Jake. No need for formalities here."

Hopefully he would leave before Izzy came out of the bedroom half naked. His ideas on formalities might be entirely different.

He slapped his hands on his thighs and stood. It occurred to me finally, that he'd arrived at my door. Even at this hour he shouldn't have been able to get past my doorman without a call to me first.

Unease began to trickle up my spine as I stood with him. He headed toward the door.

"I'll see you out," I offered.

"Thanks, that's kind of you. I'm off to see Izzy in a minute. She didn't know I was coming so I expect she will be mighty surprised."

And he will be too, when he realizes she's not at home.

I opened the door for him, holding it as he stepped across the threshold. He held his hand out once more and I grasped it to shake.

When I met his eyes, all signs of the jovial man were gone. In his place stood a steely-eyed brother about to mess up his sister's boyfriend.

"Don't worry, Mr. Gray. I already know I can't kill you. Which means this is going to be a lot more interesting."

I was sure I didn't want to know but I asked anyway. "What will be interesting?"

A sharp jolt hit my ribs and I went down to the floor. I rolled, intent on getting up, but the room spun and I flopped to my back. Jake's face hovered over mine for a flash of a second and then darkness sucked me into her cool embrace.

IZZY

The warm sun on my face woke me. I reached out my arms and rolled to my back, tingling and aching in all the good places. When I opened my eyes I sought out Gray but he wasn't in bed. The lingering scent of boiled over water on a hot stovetop hit me, and it occurred to me he might be a morning person.

Ugh, yet another strike against that sexy bastard.

I rolled over and grabbed his T-shirt off the floor. Mine had been destroyed so he'd have to survive if I borrowed his. I slipped it on and went in search of my underwear.

"I'll take some of that tea, please," I called out as I extricated the lace from my leggings and slipped them on. I spun to face him with a smile that died on my lips when I turned to find the kitchen empty.

"Gray?" I called out looking around for a flash of movement. Nothing.

A mug of tea sat on the counter, but so did his cell phone. Where could he be?

I wandered into a laundry room, the wine room, back into his bedroom for the bathroom. Even the guest room was empty.

"Where could he be?" If there was work, I'd be there too. He likely wouldn't leave without his cell phone.

I went back to the kitchen and held my hand near the kettle. It was still warm, but not hot. Then I grabbed the mug and took a sip. That wasn't even warm. And damn, that man needed to add sugar to this. I pulled the tea bag out and tossed it in the trash. So he'd been interrupted while he was drinking tea, but before he could remove the bag. That was a very short window for English Breakfast.

I looked around and caught a pad of paper and pen on the end of the counter. It hadn't been there the night before. The beautiful man had left me a note.

I picked up the creamy white notepad and scanned it. I blinked and then re-read it.

My Dearest Isobel,

If you are reading this, then I'm gone. Last night when you came to see me I had just realized I am likely going mad. I can't put you through that, nor can I expect you to care for me after our brief acquaintance. I'm going back to England, and then maybe to America, for medical care. It's likely the end and I don't want to put you through that.

Please know the few days we spent together were some of the most treasured of my life. And last night was perfect. I hope you were satisfied as well.

Hope to see you in the next life,

Love,

DG

I re-read the note a third time. "I hope you were satisfied as well." Like he was requesting a five-star rating on a delivery order. What the fuck?

I tossed the notepad on the counter and stalked through his flat once more. He wasn't there, but all of his stuff was. His books, everything. Why would he just leave it all and not say anything?

I didn't consider myself a difficult woman to talk to, or reason with. With a huff, I grabbed my wallet, keys, and phone, and headed toward the door. It was closed but not locked. He didn't even bother to lock it with me still asleep in his bed? Anger began to form in my gut, eating away all the post-orgasm euphoria. That bastard would get an earful if I ever saw him again.

Oh shit, pants.

I shimmied into them and gave his flat one last lingering glance, purposefully avoiding the entryway where he and I shared a few memories, and exited. I closed the door gently behind me and went to the elevator with a knot in my throat. Damn this hurt. Why did I put myself through this? I could have left last night when he'd asked me to a dozen times and saved myself this embarrassment and pain.

I rubbed my chest as if I could get rid of the ache there from the outside. It didn't budge. Damn bastard. I wanted to think of more colorful curse words for him but the bell dinged and I stepped inside the elevator. The lobby was empty, not even the doorman greeted me when I stepped off the elevator.

Like the whole damn building was conspiring against me.

I walked home, not wanting to even look at Michael, because he had a hand in this as well. Dragging me to Gray's place last night. And he'd been right to seek out help for his friend, but damn it, I could have woken up in my own bed, without this ache. I rubbed at it again.

You also wouldn't have had the best sex of your life last night either.

Shut up, I grumbled to myself. A passing man eyed me warily. I glared for no other reason than I wanted everyone else to feel as shitty as I did this morning.

I made it home and again crawled into my bed, letting the chemical spring-scented sheets remind me of home. And Jakey.

I shuffled my arms from under the covers and dialed his number. It took a few seconds for the usual click through but then a busy tone answered. Not once did I ever get a busy tone when he was out of town on a mission. Maybe he was trying to call me. I hung up and waited, staring at the white face for it to light up. Nothing. Absolutely nothing for twenty minutes.

I tried again. Still busy.

What the hell? I threw the phone down the bed to land in a pool of covers before tucking my arms back under and clutching the blankets to my chin.

All men were off limits today. I rolled to my back and stared at the ceiling, the movement giving me a twinge in my nether regions. Even my own body was betraying me with reminders of him.

Instead of lying in bed all day and wallowing, I shoved the covers back and went to the kitchen. My often-neglected coffee pot sat there calling my name. If Gray didn't want to be in my life, then screw him. His loss.

You didn't want him in your life first. While technically true, I shoved the thoughts away and focused on the coffee. Last night showed me we had a lot more chemistry than I'd originally expected. Dorian could be irascible and also sweet. Kind and rough. A juxtaposition I needed in a partner. And for a brief moment as I'd rolled over in his bed and remembered last night I thought he might be that partner. That would teach me for making decisions. Back to one night stands and easy lays from now on.

I grabbed a jar of Nutella and popped up on the counter to wait for the coffee to brew. Two spoonfuls in the pot hissed its completion.

The scent of the dark roast I found at a local shop warmed and cheered me a little bit. Like super-hot water, coffee was another goto perk-up method. With no parents and only my brother to raise me, and me to raise him, I'd developed whatever coping mechanisms I could to handle stress and unhappiness. And being all alone in the world from the time we were both sixteen, we'd had more than our fair share of ups and downs.

After our parents died in a plane crash, we'd lived together, in our family home, for almost six months before child protective services got us. When we were separated I thought neither of us would survive it. But we did, and we even grew into semi-productive adults. I scooped another bite of the hazelnut chocolate spread. Absolutely no dysfunction here.

It bothered me more that I couldn't get ahold of Jake than that Gray had up and run away. For a flash of a second I had thought Dorian was my Prince Charming.

When Jake and I were kids we'd play king and queen outside in our tree house. We'd rule together as brother and sister, and I would have my Prince Charming to marry, and he would have his Fairy Princess. As usual, our kingdom would be a peaceful and benevolent one. Of course, that lasted until my brother discovered video games, and I got into ballet.

That tree house was still in use by the family who bought our house at auction after we were taken away. When I'd grown brave enough to face the memories, I was happy to see the kids playing there.

The coffee let out a faint sizzle and I poured a cup before it burned from being left in the pot too long.

Not bothering with milk or sugar, I sat back on the counter and sipped it black. It suited my mood that way. Bitter and hot.

Wow, I thought. One man runs away from me and I turn into

the bitter old witch in the forest, waiting for passing children in my gingerbread house.

I decided I really wasn't going to wallow, and I finished the spoon I'd already loaded with chocolate, downed the rest of the hot coffee, and went to shower.

After that I put on makeup, got dressed, grabbed my things, and headed outside. I lived in Paris, one of the most beautiful cities in the world. And after *Romeo and Juliet* in a few weeks, maybe I'd take a job in another city to get away from the memories here. I should savor the ankle-breaking cobblestone streets while I could.

I headed the opposite direct of my home, and Gray's, as well as the theater. When I first arrive in a new city I spend a lot of time wandering, getting lost, figuring out how to get where I needed. Today, I did it for the pleasure of it. I wandered the city's tunnels and avenues until the memory of Gray was so far in the back of my mind I could barely remember the damnable spicy cologne that made me want to bite him.

A bookstore caught my eye, but as I ran my fingers across the spines I saw Gray sitting on his living room floor holding a stack of books.

"Get your shit together, woman. He is one man, you spent a few days together. Get over it." Talking to myself probably isn't a good sign.

I sighed and continued on, not going in for fear he would haunt me more inside the shop.

My favorite stationary store sat on the corner a few blocks down, so I decided to head there. The heavenly scent of fresh baked bread reached me from across the street so now I had two absolutely non-Gray related stops I could make.

I went inside the stationary store first and puttered around pen racks and stacks of notebooks. On the back wall, books lined a tall shelf. Lovely, leather-bound journals. I petted the spines of those as well, which were already developing a beautiful patina from other customers. I had no need for journaling or I might have been tempted.

I bought a few pens, some fountain pen refill ink, and crossed the street to the bread shop. As I entered, I tripped over the step in the doorway and fell right into a man's arms. He caught me by the elbows and helped me stand. I glanced up to say thank you only to jerk back. "Hello, Mikey."

"Hello, Miss." He smiled but I scowled. The smile slowly fell from his lips. "What have I done?"

"I thought you'd be with Gray right now," I said, instead of answering his question.

He chuckled. "I thought he would still be with you right now."

I shifted the bag of supplies to my purse and rubbed my hands together, cracking the knuckles, a habit I couldn't get rid of when my anxiety was high. "If you didn't take him somewhere, and he's not with me, where is he?"

DORIAN

I awoke shivering in a dark room, water dripping somewhere behind me. The last thing I remembered was the sharp bite in my abdomen. Still in my pants, I glanced down and spotted two angry red circles in the middle of my waist. Damn Tasers, definitely not a new invention I appreciated.

"You're awake."

I glanced up toward my captor standing in the doorway. Jake, Izzy's brother.

Izzy.

Her face flashed before my eyes. What must she have thought of me as she woke this morning alone?

"You have no right to hold me here. This is kidnapping."

He chuckled and leaned on the doorframe. "I won't keep you long. Just long enough."

"For what?"

"To talk some sense into you."

I gestured at the Taser marks on my stomach. "And you had to do this? You couldn't chat with me in my living room over tea like civilized men?"

He entered the room and closed the door. I stood thinking I was probably about to have to defend myself. In all my years, fighting was never a skill I wanted to learn. I could throw a punch when necessary but I'd never gone out of my way to learn the various styles that passed in and out of fashion through the years.

"Sit down, I don't intend to hurt you, yet." He threw himself in a metal chair off to the side of the cot I woke up on.

"What do you want with me? Are you even Izzy's brother or did you use that as a ruse to get to me?"

He shifted forward so his elbows braced on top of his thighs and narrowed his eyes. "What do you think?"

I scanned his features. Their eyes were the same and yet different. It disconcerted me I couldn't get an accurate read on him, as I was usually very good at that sort of thing.

He waited and I didn't answer, which I supposed he took for not knowing. "I am Izzy's brother. My name is Jake, as I mentioned."

"So, what is this about? Did the Americans decide I'm a threat again, and send you to bring me in?"

He shook his head and then let it hang down. "No, this is all personal."

I failed to see the logic in his plan. How was this meant to play out? "Are you intending to threaten me into staying away from your sister? I assure you, I already tried pushing her away and it failed spectacularly."

The press of her hands on my chest flashed in my head. I dropped my gaze so he couldn't see that there. It was mine. She was mine.

He stood and scooted his chair closer, so only a foot of space lay between our knees. I tried to stop the shiver in mine from the chilly room. "I have no intention of threatening you. You're going to stay away from her all on your own."

"And how is that?"

Anger was replacing any sense of honor I had in dealing with her brother. Kidnapping people, tasing them, that was the action of a lunatic. That sort of person didn't deserve my respect, no matter who his relations were.

He reached around and pulled out an envelope from his back pocket. I watched carefully in case he had some sort of needle or weaponized powder stashed inside. He pulled up the flap and lifted out a piece of paper. It had already been folded and refolded several times. I glanced between the paper and his eyes, waiting for the answer. Each action he made was slow, precise, and deliberate. I had no doubt this was his end game. Something I was supposed to realize.

He opened the paper, folded horizontally in three parts, and handed it to me. It was an old picture, a photocopy of a painting. The style was from the era when I was born and by the shape and size it looked to be a miniature. A small, framed portrait people had made to give to family or potential spouses in my day.

"Why are you showing me this?"

He pointed to the paper. "Do you recognize her?"

I scanned her features, trying to associate something with my past or my memory. Nothing. I didn't recognize a single thing about the girl. "No, I'm afraid I don't know who she is."

"Look again."

I glanced back down, my patience running out. "No, I don't know her."

He smiled, it was the smile of a man who had just delivered a check mate. The one given just before a killing blow. "That is Sibyl Vane."

I replayed his words in my head and glanced back down to the image on the page. The woman had brown hair like I recall Sibyl having, but this round faced-creature stirred no memory in me. "This isn't Sibyl."

"It is," he said. "I assure you, I have impeccable sources."

I flicked the paper at him and he let it fall to the floor between us, not even flinching to grasp it out of the air. "You may have sources, but I was there. I knew her personally. That's not her."

He pulled another piece of paper from the envelope, a small gray square, and I snatched it from him to look.

The obituary spoke about Sibyl, but I don't remember having ever seen an obituary for her. The image in the painting was exactly the same as the girl in a photo accompanying the article.

I stared at it, rereading for as long as I dared. When I looked back up, Jake sat watching me carefully. "Do you recognize her now?"

I shook my head. "I've never seen this woman in my life."

What did that mean? Was I never acquainted with Sibyl? Or perhaps the woman I knew was someone impersonating her?"

No, that was impossible too. I met her the first time after she performed on stage. I folded over and clutched my head in my hands.

"I don't understand."

The chair in front of me shifted and the paper was scooped from the floor. I glanced up to him holding his cell phone out to me. I took it, uncertain what else he wanted to show me.

The image on his screen was Izzy. Her short blonde hair, that wide smile that could drop me to my knees. She looked so beautiful, so happy, in that picture. "Do you know who that is?"

"It's Izzy."

He nodded. "Well, you're one for two, at least."

I opened my arms, surrendering to whatever game he was playing. "What do you want from me? Why am I here?"

He shook his head and slipped his phone into his cargo pocket. "You're here until you realize that being with my sister is detrimental to her health and happiness. You're not a sane man, Mr. Gray."

"What do you even know about me? Who the hell are you?"

"My name is Warrant Officer Jake Vale. Isobel is my sister. That's all you really need to know about me. And more than most do."

"I'm going to ask you again, what do you want with me?"

He leaned in, his face only inches from mine. I could see Izzy's eyes and it threw me off even more. "Do you recognize me at all?"

"You and your sister share eyes."

"That's not all we share. Izzy and I are identical twins. I was born two minutes before she was."

I scanned his face but it was like trying to turn on a light when the bulb had blown. I couldn't line his features up with Izzy's and make them fit.

"You don't see it, do you? It's because you're not well. I spoke to the medical team that treats you, Gray. They confirmed your symptoms already. You'll start seeing things, inverting memories and faces, until the past and present mix up and you will be unable to untangle the two. Apparently, it's common once a patient passes the hundred-year mark. It's the start of your mental deterioration."

I let his words sink in. Hadn't I considered the very same possibility? But Sibyl and Izzy? I'd only sought Izzy out because she looked so much like Sibyl, hadn't she? And now, after seeing those images of Sibyl, it was fresh in my mind that they looked nothing alike. Then there was Izzy and her brother, who also looked nothing alike to me.

"Did the doctors tell you how to fix it?"

He shifted in the chair, causing it to squeak some more under his weight. "They advised you go stay at their center for treatment. Do you understand why I'm doing this, Gray? My sister cares about you.

Once she told me about you, I showed up within hours to keep watch over her. I can see that she cares for you and I know you care for her. If you truly do, then you will let her go so you can get the medical help you need."

I thought about Izzy, how angry she must be waking up to find me gone. "I can't just leave her without so much as a goodbye."

He waved his hand like a magician presenting a new trick. "You already took care of that too. That note you left on the counter was very effective."

I remembered writing her the note, but I could barely recall the words. The most important part was that she thought I left her, just up and left without a word.

Damn. I did intend to leave, didn't I? I knew something was wrong already, maybe subconsciously, a little bit more.

"Let me take you to get treatment," Jake said.

I met his eyes and let him see the anger I'd been keeping at bay. "I will not be going anywhere with you. What I do with my life and with whom is none of your concern, even if she is your sister. She is an adult and can make her own choices."

"Wait a…"

"No," I stood up and tried to muster all the dignity I usually possessed in my bespoke suits while still in my boxer briefs. "You are letting me out of this rat cage and you will give me some clothes. Talking about your sister, my health, all of it...not a single thing warranted being tased, kidnapped, and locked up like a prisoner."

He rubbed his neck and had the gall to look sheepish now. "Some of it may have been for my benefit. I know you're fucking my twin sister and I don't appreciate it."

"She's a grown woman and if I know her, if she knew about this she'd have your balls in a bell jar under her sink."

He laughed, and for the first time I could see her in his face. That smile was just like hers. "Well, you do know her, I'll give you that. I don't intend to tell her about all this. And if you tell her it will only hurt her more. You should get out and away while she thinks you're just gone. A clean exit is open for you, just take it, Gray."

I had no intention of taking advice from this man. In fact, I had no intention of saying another word until I was properly showered, fed, and clothed. "Take me home now."

He nodded and stood up. I watched him carefully before following him to the door. "I'm sorry about this," he said.

I thought he meant the kidnapping and lecture. But, he actually meant the pistol whip he gave me to the back of the head.

IZZY

THE MAN ACROSS FROM ME was not Dorian Gray. In fact, he couldn't be Dorian Gray on even his best day. I tilted my head to stare at him at a different angle, hoping it would help. Nope. Nothing.

Currently he was on his fourth tirade about the American healthcare system. The first time I pretended to be interested. Now I wished the table was bigger so I could hide my phone under the edge to play Candy Crush. At least until I could make a quick clean getaway.

After I saw Michael yesterday he assured me Dorian often went off on his own and that I shouldn't worry. He actually shooed me out of the pastry shop and onto the street…without a loaf of bread.

It didn't stop the worry though. Especially because Jake had yet to call me back. He always called me within at least an hour of me contacting him. This radio silence made me fear the worst.

The world thinks twins have a sort of psychic connection. Not in my experience. Jake and I may look alike, and we definitely love each other, but we also couldn't be more different.

I defined impulsiveness; him, logic and reason. He was always the military man and patriotic solider. I'm more of the wild-child artist. I resisted the urge to pull my phone out, instead taking a long slow drink of my coffee so I could stop smiling and nodding at this guy for a second.

What was his name? Rob, Ron, Rich…I think it started with an R.

Someone from the theater came into the café and waved. I seized on that gesture and waved back, standing and giving Rob, Rob, Rich a give-me-one-second hand. When I reached the woman, I stopped and waited silently.

She leaned to glance at my table. "Are you alright? Do I need to call the cops or something?"

I shook my head. "No please just stand here and look really concerned so I can stay here plausibly for a few minutes."

She chuckled and ordered her coffee then schooled her features into a frown. "Is it that bad? Come on."

"Oh I just learned more about insurance companies than I ever needed or wanted to know."

"Why insurance companies?"

I shook my head. "Also something I really don't want to know."

The barista gave her the coffee and she turned to go. "Please, stay, chat. How's the boyfriend?" I begged.

She took a sip. "I don't have a boyfriend. Although I hear you do, and it's not the insurance sales man over there."

"Ok, Trish, back to work!"

I whooshed her away with my arms before I returned to the small table. "Sorry about that, work thing."

He nodded and launched right back in where he'd stopped before I left. I lasted five more minutes before I pretended my phone was vibrating in my pocket and I had to go. He leaned in to kiss my cheek and I had to talk myself into keeping my feet planted to let him.

This is why I don't date. Damn it, Gray. I was pissed when I'd realized we had something good before we even got to explore the options. I was pissed he left without saying a word to me about it. I was pissed that I cared so damn much that I wasn't sleeping well.

As I stepped out of the café my phone did start vibrating. Unknown number. I swiped the screen. "Hello?"

"Hey, Beautiful."

All the air pushed out of me like a sharp poke to an overinflated balloon. "Jake. You asshole, why haven't you called?"

"Sorry, Iz, I've been busy. I didn't mean to worry you."

I tried to keep some of the shaking from my voice while I clutched the phone in both hands to my ear. "I wasn't worried. More like scared I'd have to adopt your cat if you died. That thing hates me."

"Uh huh, I'm sure that was it."

"Okay but really, are you alright? Is 'busy' code for classified or…"

"I actually can't talk about it right now, Iz. But I'll fill you in really soon."

"How soon?" I whined. "I miss you and I haven't talked to you in what feels like days."

He laughed, that comforting magical warm laugh. "It's been like forty-eight hours Iz, calm down."

I walked slowly toward my apartment and conceded. "Ok, fine. But I expect you to call me back soon."

"See you soon, Iz."

He hung up and I stopped to spend a moment frowning at my phone like it was to blame. No, it was me. I'd been in a mood since Gray left and then my brother wasn't calling. Like everything conspired against me at once. Even the actors at the theater were trying to test my patience at every turn. Constantly complaining about rehearsing at the studio space instead of the theater. Like I could fix the flooding and mold issues.

Romeo had already threatened to quit twice and Josephine... I massaged my temples at the thought of my ultra-diva. If Josephine didn't stop throwing up after every meal, there wouldn't be anything left of her to fit into the costume on opening night. I'd taken to trapping her in a scene after she ate on set so that she couldn't get away to puke. It wasn't the drama; it was that I didn't know what to do to help her beat her illness. I'm a producer and so not equipped for that.

As I walked home, I thought about Jake. He'd always seemed so solid in his choices. The military all the way and then when he got into the Navy SEALs it was the same level of joy as when I was asked to come to Paris to work with the theater. But I didn't feel that same sense of commitment he did. Every night I wondered if I was meant to be something else, do something else, go somewhere else.

It was never about the job. I loved producing plays. And no matter how much work or drama went into creating a play, opening night always somehow fell together. Almost by divine ordinance.

Once the crowd stands and cheers, tears often shining in some eyes, I'd get that overwhelming sense that the stage is where I belong.

But outside of that single shining victory I often wondered why the hell I put myself through traveling around the globe, dealing with sick and insane actors, also the occasional billionaire or two. No one was ever like Gray though. Something about him felt different. More comfortable, like my brother, solid and certain in his convictions and character.

I wanted that level of certainty in my life. Instead I moved all over, dated men who didn't call, friends who didn't call…hell, no one ever called when they were supposed to.

A sense of melancholy lingered and I could feel it's dark grip trying to lull me in a deep funk. Usually they lasted a couple days. I was not going to let Dorian Gray throw me into that mess. No.

I marched all the way home thinking about donuts, fresh coffee, and Dorian's mouth on my neck. It was sad to think about him being gone but the time we shared had been lovely. No doubts about that.

I made it to my apartment and focused only on the good things. Coffee came first. I dropped my bag on the countertop and shuffled around the kitchen to brew a cup. In the mood for something bitter, I found my dark roast and started the hot water.

At least I could do coffee right.

My phone vibrated inside my bag and I snatched it out of the opening before it could tumble out on the granite. Another unknown caller.

"Jake?" I answer.

"I told you I'd talk to you soon."

"You're such an idiot. You could have just told me you call me back in a minute."

I hopped up on the counter and swung my legs to knock my heels against the cabinet. "So, tell me what's been going on. Why haven't you been able to call?"

"Well, I can't tell you everything but I can tell you that I've been traveling. That's why I wasn't able to call you back before. I'm actually in another country now."

"Yeah? Which one?"

Static and shuffling came through. "Jake?"

"Iz, you know I can't tell you anything that specific."

"I know, just testing your commitment to our national security, of course."

He laughed. Oh I missed hearing that laugh in person. "When will you get to take leave? Maybe you can come visit and we can go to the wine country or to the beach."

"Which beach do you want to go to?"

I shrugged even though he couldn't see me. "I don't know, but I'm sure between our super smart selves we can find one far enough away. Hell, we can take a train to Italy, where I know there's at least a thousand miles between here and us."

Another laugh. "You know how I love those Italians."

I shook my head and rolled my eyes.

"Wasn't your last boyfriend Italian?"

"And my last girlfriend. They were a couple actually. Happy to take in a lonely soldier on leave traveling alone for the holiday." His tone was all innocence and sweet male guile.

"You're incorrigible."

"Hey, we all got what we wanted out of the bargain. No complaints on any side. They both call me from time to time and invite me back."

"Back to where?"

"Tuscany. Excellent wine there, too."

I shifted on the counter and tucked my feet up under my legs. "Okay then it sounds like we have a plan. You just need to take some leave and get your butt to France."

He made a noise like he was considering his choices. "I don't know Iz, it's kind of hot in France this time of year."

"Not any hotter than Italy, dork."

"Okay, okay, I guess I'll get myself to France. It has been a while since you and I spent any real time together. Of course, after we visit you might not want me anywhere near you for a while."

"Huh? What does that mean?"

A soft knock came at my door. "Hold on Jake I'm going to put the phone down, someone is knocking."

I set the phone on the counter, hopped off the edge, and went to the door. I didn't have a peephole but my doorman was supposed to ring me if anyone showed up. Come to think of it he'd been failing at that task for some time.

I opened the door and froze.

"Hello, Sis."

IZZY

I BLINKED TRYING TO CLEAR the tears from my eyes. They slid down my cheeks in hot streams as I threw myself into Jake's arms. He wrapped himself around me, pulling me close. He smelled like Jake, my Jakey. The only family I had.

I pulled back for a second just to look at his face before burying my ear into his chest again as I squeezed him tight.

"Let's go inside, Iz," he said, gently walking me backward into my home and then closing the door behind him.

I leaned away from him. "You bastard, don't toy with my emotions like that." I punched him in the shoulder so he'd remember next time.

He let me go and I reluctantly let him go too. "What are you doing here?"

Instead of crowding around the door I led him into the kitchen and grabbed another coffee mug from the cabinet. He watched me, smiling. "What?"

"Nothing," he said, shaking his head at the same time. "It's just been a while since I've seen you. I missed you, Little Sis."

I poured coffee in both mugs and then handed him the other. He never took cream or sugar, drinking it black like I did sometimes.

After he took a couple tentative sips he backtracked to sit on the stool off my small kitchen bar. "Sorry I couldn't tell you I was coming. You know they don't let us talk about when we are traveling or where."

"What if I was busy, or if you came on opening night?"

He smiled and I wanted to touch the deep dimple in his cheeks. "Not a chance. I know you better than anyone, and I know your schedule. Opening night is a couple weeks away still. Besides, I'm not here for long. Only today. Then I have to get back to work."

"Only today? The day's almost gone. Why didn't you come by this morning?"

He bit his lip and I knew something was wrong. "What is it, Jake?"

When he sat the mug down and rubbed his hands across the tops of his thighs, and I knew something was really wrong. "Jake, you're starting to scare me."

"Maybe you should put that coffee down," he said before he swiveled on the stool and gestured for me to take the other one.

Once I'd settled I eyed him warily. He pushed my bag and things toward the other end of the counter, out of reach. "Jake, what did you do?"

He released a long heavy sigh and shifted toward me so our knees lined up. He was the same height as me so I could meet his eyes square on. They looked frightened.

"Jake, what did you do?" I asked again with a little more force.

Seconds passed in heavy silence. I didn't recall him every giving me this look of apprehension and shame.

"You know that guy you asked me to look into?"

Dread began to build in my belly but I held it with tight reigns, praying Jake didn't kill him or worse.

"Well, I learned something about him. Then after I sent you his details I saw that you deleted the email without even looking at the pdf file."

"Yes, I deleted it. He told me everything I wanted to know."

"He didn't tell you everything, Izzy."

"Okay, so what? We've known each other a very short time. I don't expect to know all his secrets right off the bat. Especially since I wasn't entirely sure I wanted to be with him. I wanted to keep things casual."

"They didn't look casual, Izzy."

My mouth dropped open and I clamped it shut once I realized. "Have you been spying on me?"

"I got on a plane after our conversation. I've been spying on Gray, not you."

I wanted to slap him. My own twin brother, treating me like a child. "I'm a thirty-year-old woman for fuck's sake. I don't need you to rough up my boyfriend, or sex partners, for me."

He flinched at the word sex partner and I knew he would. I'd thrown it in there just to torture him. "What did you do, Jake? Besides betray my trust?"

I slid off the stool and began to pace alongside the bar. If I sat and looked at him the entire time he recounted his story I might murder him. And the cleanup would be hell. The big question echoing in my head was why he felt the need for such a dramatic step. I'd had many boyfriends, and even sex partners, in the past. He'd never flown around the world, or wherever, to spy on them.

"Why did you do this?" I asked, not looking at his face, still pacing.

"I only did it because this guy is insane. And I'm not talking normal person insane, actual freaking certifiably insane. You didn't read the report and I was worried, so I came out to make sure you were alright."

"By stalking the guy I was sleeping with. How does that tell you if I'm alright?"

He shifted off the stool and pulled a squished roll of white paper from his pocket. I snatched it out of his hand with a glower.

The papers had a bunch of test result numbers printed on them. I read as I paced back and forth, barely catching some of the scientific jargon underneath an assessment, "I don't know what this says, Jake. Just explain it to me."

He shifted forward, sliding both feet off the rungs of the stool onto the floor. "It means your boyfriend's brain has reached its breaking point. He's been hallucinating. All the crap about him thinking you're the reincarnation of that girl he killed, none of it's true. You don't look anything like her. His mind is breaking and he latched on to you as some sort of reality handle."

I narrowed my eyes and stepped back from my brother. The one solid foundation I'd possessed my entire life seemed to be crumbling around the edges. It wasn't all this crap about Gray that bothered me. It was him being in my city without telling me, without coming to me.

Him lying about where he was and not calling. Him stalking the guy I was sleeping with. None of it made any damn sense.

I shoved the papers at his chest. "This doesn't matter. I told you. He and I were seeing each other and now we are not. You've done a dumb ass thing for absolutely no reason. And now I'm mad at you."

Damn him for being such a pig-headed male like all the rest of them. He was supposed to be the different one. The one I could count on. I grabbed my mug and refilled it with hot coffee to warm up the liquid that remained in my cup. Jake sat with his back to me, his head hanging down as he lined up the papers and rolled them back up to put in his pocket again.

When he finished he spun around on the stool to face me again.

"What?" I asked. "Did you decide it's time to tell me our dog Champ didn't actually go to doggy heaven? Because guess what, I know that too."

He rolled his eyes and propped his elbows on the counter top. "Stop being so dramatic."

"I'm the dramatic one?" Anger threatened to turn the volume of my next tirade up a notch, until I met his eyes. "Damn it, Jake. That's not all, is it? You did more stupid crap you're afraid to tell me about."

He swallowed and stared down at his clasped hands. Avoiding

eye contact, even better. "I sort of tased your boyfriend and then kidnapped him for questioning."

If he'd told me that he spent his weekends skinny-dipping in the Baltic Ocean I wouldn't have been more shocked. Every time he'd threatened to kidnap and murder the men in my life I'd taken it as a joke. Never had I ever considered he'd actually hurt one of them. Outside of the situation in which they hurt me first.

"Are you joking?" I asked, trying to remain calm. Voice steady and low. Just like when the actors were being fussy diva four-year-olds.

"No. I wish I was, because I know how angry you are right now. I promise it wasn't the plan at all. It sort of happened."

I lurched around the counter and grabbed his shoulders tight, shaking him. He finally met my eyes. "You sort of brought a taser with you one day and sort of just kidnapped him?"

He slid his gaze away. "It was the morning you were sleeping at his place. I knocked on the door, we talked, and then he was in the trunk of my car passed out."

I let him go and stepped back. "I don't even know what to say to you right now. Where is he?"

He shrugged. "After we talked I gave him some clothes and let him go. I presume he went to speak to the scientists he works with for his…problem. Or maybe he went to find proof of that girl."

"Sibyl? What do you know about her?"

Sensing that he was gaining traction on safer ground, he kept going. "Like I said before. This girl he thinks was you in a past life, she is nothing like you, she doesn't look like you or anything. Something is going on with his memories. They're overlapping like seismic plates trying to create room. The resulting earthquakes are messing with his perception of his reality."

I blinked. "How did you…"

He shrugged. "I made some calls and got the information. I didn't want to risk leaving you alone with him."

"So obviously, kidnapping is the way to go." I went to my mug and turned my back to him while I sipped it. If Dorian wasn't being held hostage, why didn't he call? It took two full seconds for the rational part of my brain to catch up. Obviously he was going through something serious right now. He didn't need to call me while he handled something like that. In fact, I might have found it worse if he did.

"Iz?" Jake broached.

I didn't turn. "I am not talking to you right now. Sit there and be quiet for a minute while I think."

The smart man did as he was told.

I wished I had a way to get a hold of him to let him know I was here if he needed me. Sex or no sex, I did want to be friends with him. We had incredible chemistry but also he made me laugh and feel things that weren't everyday life sort of feelings. Joy, lust that melted your bones. Everything with him felt deeper and more meaningful. I didn't want to lose that, even if it went the platonic route.

I don't know how long I stood facing my refrigerator, but eventually I turned to catch Jake leaning on his elbow on top of the counter.

"Is that it? Any other revelations to deliver? Are you undergoing a sex change next week or anything?"

He chuckled, and even mad at him I reveled in the comfort of his laugh.

He said, "Not that I'm aware of, but if I do I'll be back to borrow your clothes." He stood and I let him hug me, wrapping his arms tight around my shoulders.

It seemed like both of the men I wanted in my life might drive me slowly insane. I thought back to Gray. If it was true and I'm not anything like Sibyl, would he still want me? Or did he only want me because he thought I was a second chance for him?

Jake felt the shift in my body. "What is it?" he asked.

I pulled back. "Nope. We aren't talking about any of this or I'm going to get pissed all over again. For now, you're here and we are going to spend an enjoyable evening before you head to some unidentifiable sandbox in God-knows-where."

He jerked me in for another hug, my coffee sloshed down the side of my hand, and I didn't care.

"Oh, he asked me to give you a letter."

Jake pulled a folded envelope from his other pants pocket and handed it to me.

"You didn't open it?"

He snorted. "I know you better than that. I want to keep my balls in place, thank you."

DORIAN

I sat on the countertop in my kitchen for an hour, maybe two, I couldn't tell, between the kidnapping and the return trip home. My clothes smelled like a locker room and the two red dots on my abs burned with every breath I took. A few more hours and they'd fade to nothing.

Jake may be a very nice man, but I hoped to never see him again. There would be words and likely fists involved. I couldn't imagine what his sister would say when she learned of his actions. It was almost—almost enough to make me feel sorry for him.

Izzy's fingerprints were smudged beside the handle on the refrigerator. When she cooked me dinner she must have touched it.

What I couldn't stop studying was the shape and length of the hazy ovals. She was taller than I thought Sibyl was. Her hands were larger, still smaller than my own, but larger than Sibyl's too.

I'd considered my mental deterioration over the years, and more and more as of late. This new scare had me on edge. Torn between going to the States to visit the doctors and walking to Izzy's house, I opted for neither. So I sat on the counter, in the same spot she'd occupied, and I waited until my mind came up with a plan that wouldn't hurt her, or me, irrevocably.

My phone rang, the shrill *brrring* shattered the silence of my home and pushed me further toward hysteria.

I swiped my finger across the face and answered. "Hello?"

"Dorian," Michael said my name on an exhale. "Thank goodness, I wasn't sure where you were and then Ms. Vale told me you left. I was worried."

"My apologies for your concern, but I'm fine."

"You don't sound fine; in fact, you sound a little out of it. What happened?"

"It's too much to explain over the phone and I'm not really in the mood. Can I contact you later and we can chat?"

"Sure, yeah, of course."

I hung up without saying goodbye. He'd have heard how much effort it took to say that as well. For now, I needed to be alone. If everyone stayed away they would be safe. If Izzy stayed away she would be safe.

How did one test for insanity? I could go to the local mental hospital, but that would likely yield the same results as heading to Dr. Robertson's office in America. Incarceration until death didn't appeal to me.

Was it all true? Had I imagined that Izzy looked like Sibyl? Was our entire attraction a figment of my decaying mind?

It couldn't all be, not with Izzy giving herself to me in the ways she did. In two of the three interactions we'd had she had turned over control to me. That spoke of something deeper than delusion.

Tired of the sweat-stained clothes smell emanating from me I hopped off the counter and headed for the shower. Once I got Jake's Navy workout gear off I tossed it in the trash and walked back to the already steaming water. As it cascaded from the rainfall shower head, I let my mind drift back to her. Even in the short time we'd been apart I missed her like I'd lost a vital organ. What did that say about our relationship? Was it a true feeling or something I associated with her because of Sibyl?

I had to still my thoughts and shower one item at a time to avoid going down a rabbit hole I couldn't climb out of. Once I wore my own clothes again I felt like I could think on my own again too. It did wonders for improving my mood. Coffee and food next. I texted Michael instead of calling him and he agreed to send food up via the doorman. I ordered an omelet, bacon, and fresh-pressed coffee.

Money made things move fast and I paid more than the meal was worth to get it delivered in under a half hour. Alone again with my food I spent the next twenty minutes only focusing on the task of eating. As soon as I allowed my thoughts to stray everything went haywire.

Though it was more like the second Izzy came to mind nothing else could get in. Damn that woman and her doe eyes and…I slapped my utensils on the counter, grabbed my cup of coffee, and went to sit on the couch.

My flat in disarray would usually throw more fire on the kerosene of my volatile mood but it would seem I'd ignited a bonfire, and anything added to it was inconsequential.

Coffee in hand, I swiveled and shifted until I sank into the soft leather of my couch. I allowed it to cocoon me and let me float on a caffeine cloud as I came up with a plan. There were priorities to consider.

Don't hurt Izzy was the first. The note I'd written was gone and she likely saw it. So the first priority probably didn't matter. Unless Jake confessed to his part in my disappearance. He loved his sister but I wasn't sure he would actually tell her. I'd spent a brief time with him and read absolutely nothing from his face besides the similarities to Izzy's.

Why hadn't she told me he was her twin brother? If he went out of his way to kidnap his sister's lover what else could he be capable of?

Seeing her, even if she hated me, still felt like the right thing to do. I couldn't visit her in my current state. Right now I appeared more bum than billionaire. If it was the last time we saw each other I didn't want that to be the memory she held onto.

No, I decided I'd see her opening night of *Romeo and Juliet*. It could be a test of sorts. That was the last play I saw Sibyl in. The words, the atmosphere, having Izzy there, would all be the perfect test of my mental faculties.

What if it went *Phantom of the Opera* wrong though? Her safety was the most important part of it all.

I considered trying to find her unhinged brother to protect her while I saw her, but he would likely turn me away. Michael would accompany me, but he wasn't the kind of man for a fight. I made a list of my friends in my mind, and found it shorter than I thought. I only trusted a handful of people in the entire world with my secrets, and not even all of them. Each person had their own special version of my story. Izzy, who I'd know the least amount of time, held the most of it.

The smart thing to do would be to go into the hospital. It had been a year since I'd last visited. Every time I went they bragged about being close to something that could help. After almost sixty years of the same speech I had my doubts. Perhaps it was time to ask them outright if they were close.

I closed my eyes and leaned my head on the back of the cushion. Izzy's face swam before my mind. It wasn't Izzy I was getting confused with Sibyl, it was my memory of Sibyl that had been misplaced. But I feared Jake having told Izzy everything would make her wonder if I still wanted her. If maybe I'd only been with her because of Sibyl.

It might have started out that way, but the more time I spent with her the less I thought of Sibyl and the more I just wanted Izzy.

That fire and energy she lived with each day was astounding to witness. Every arm gesture, every sip of her coffee, they were all fraught with an overextended sense of wonder. Sibyl, while beautiful, had only ever been remarkable while she was onstage acting. Otherwise, her character was meek and agreeable. I preferred Izzy's fight every time.

I dragged my phone from the pocket of my flannel pants and opened the text message application. Izzy's name was at the top of my contacts as a favorite. I punched the button and hovered my fingers over the miniscule digital letters. What did I say to her? Did I apologize or grovel? Should I simply send her flowers? No. She didn't seem like an apology bouquet sort of woman.

I typed, the keys faux-clicking along with each press:

> Isobel. I have returned home. Please don't come.
> I just wanted you to know I'm well.

A minute passed before I built the courage to hit send. It left with a whooshing noise and I clicked the button to darken the screen again.

I could only pray she heeded my request and stayed away. If she showed up I didn't know if I could keep myself away from her. I'd already proven how well that could work.

My phone pinged and I stared at the green box that had popped up on the screen. The text from Izzy read:

> This isn't over, Gray.

Only that damn woman would convey her concern with a threat. I appreciated that about her. The crass way she could throw around words to make people flinch while knowing the entire Shakespeare bibliography by heart.

She wielded her words to strike, cut, and sting. Some might even call it a gift; at least those who weren't on the pointy end of her barbs.

I slid the box so that it wouldn't continue to ping and wondered if she was on her way to me right now to deliver a scolding.

With a sigh I put my cup and phone down. The massive pile of books in the middle of my living room needed rectifying.

I sank to the floor and began organizing the same way I had when Izzy had helped. This time I wasn't interrupted by revelations of insanity. That was the thing about being crazy. Once you're there, it doesn't matter. There wasn't anywhere further you could go after that.

I slid the books together, lining up the spines on the carpet in alphabetical order so that I could transfer them over to the shelves more easily. One blasted book fell over from the stack and I sat it back up. It was ironic that it was the one volume I wanted least to touch. Why had I kept it all these years? By now the immaculate first edition was worth a fortune. But this one was tear stained by the author. Delivered by courier. If the truth ever came out it would likely double in value.

I remembered the knock on my door. Wait. A knock actually did come from my door. I shifted out of my piles, careful not to jostle anything over and went for the handle.

When I jerked it open I expected to see Izzy standing on the other side. Instead, an envelope sat propped against my doorframe. I recognized the stationary. The front had my last name scribbled across it: Gray.

I slipped the gold filigree card from the slot and tried to clear my mind again.

An invitation.

Romeo and Juliet to be performed at my theater in one week.

One week to prepare.

One week to elude a mental breakdown.

One week to figure out how to make Isobel mine for good.

IZZY

I DIDN'T KNOW WHY I invited him to opening night. To be fair, all he had to do was walk in the door; he didn't actually need an invitation to attend. I'd delivered it more as a warning that he and I would figure this out. I'd given him a week, and I was curious to see what he did with it.

The play went off without a hitch. As I knew it would. I only hired the best, and despite the drama and adversity we fought through during rehearsal and with the theater renovations, I'd known we would pull through.

I couldn't focus on Gray until after the play. With everyone standing in the Grand Foyer in black tie, I scanned the crowd for him.

Above me the gold ornate statuary and paintings glowed in the faux candlelight. This place must have been magical with real candlelight. Or maybe just hot.

The sponsors always celebrated opening night with a party. And the board loved any excuse to get the sponsors drunk enough to part with their checkbooks.

I skirted the edge of the room, not wanting to be drawn into any more congratulatory speeches that ended with a man congratulating me on a triumph, and complimenting himself.

But really it was the best vantage point from which to look for Gray. As one of the board members and the owner of the theater he should be here.

Once I got tired of circling in my too-high heels I braced myself against a column and waited. Any second I'd catch a glimpse…

"You know this place had a serious candle budget back in the day."

His voice caressed my skin like warm velvet.

"I was just wondering how warm it would get in here if there were thousands of lit candles overhead and circling the room."

He stepped up to the opposite side of the column and I hazarded a peek at him. Exactly the same as the last time I saw him, and yet his face looked a little leaner. His smile appeared forced and strained. But

I doubted anyone would pick that up. At least not anyone in this room.

He wore a black tuxedo, black shirt, black bowtie, and even his shoes were black. The color did very good things for him. I swallowed the naughty turn to my thoughts and smoothed out the deep royal blue of my dress. The sweetheart neckline bared my shoulders and décolletage; I'd chosen the dress purposefully to get Gray's attention. I'd even skipped dinner so didn't ruin the beautiful satin before he had a chance to see it.

"It would be very hot. And the clothes were all higher quality, thicker fabrics, with so many layers you couldn't get dressed without help. So even more warm because of that."

I crossed my arms under my breasts and pushed off the column to face him. "I owe you an apology."

His mouth hung open as if he were about to say something and he snapped it shut after my declaration.

"I'm sorry my brother kidnapped you and forced you to listen to one of his boring lectures."

"I think…"

"Oh and I'm sorry he tased you. That really wasn't cool. To be fair, he did say Chloroform hurts more and it takes a lot longer to work than tasing so that is why he chose that…" I trailed off. He likely didn't need the rundown I'd forced out of Jake before he left.

He blinked a few times and stepped forward enough that I could smell his cologne. I wanted to press my face to his neck and snort it. The smell reminded me of his hands on my body and his teeth. All of it.

I stepped forward, closing the distance between us but not touching him. "Can we get out of here and talk?"

He nodded and held out his elbow. I threaded my arm through the loop he created and he clasped my forearm against his body tight. "Now you can't escape," he teased.

Little did he know I was thinking the same thing.

Outside the ornate front doors, which no one in the company ever used, about a quarter of the guests milled around. Some were smoking; others sat stretching their legs out on the stairs. One couple was hot and heavy around the bend of a statue.

Dorian guided me along and I allowed him to lead me wherever he wanted to go. We stayed silent. I figured he wanted privacy and the square and side streets were packed with people after the event. I was surprised when we ended up at my front door.

I led him in and slipped off the shoes that had begun blisters on my heels. Luckily, before Band-Aids were required. Blood and satin are not a good combination.

He hovered awkwardly by the door. As if he wanted to make a dash whenever the first opportunity arose.

I pointed to the couch. "You can sit down."

He sat on the edge of my couch and tested its give. It must have performed well because he sank back into it with a sigh.

"Are your shoes killing you too? You're welcome to take them off."

He chuckled and just like that it felt normal, being here in my home with him. "No, I have some experience with uncomfortable footwear."

I threw myself down on the couch beside him in a cloud of satin and crinoline. Once I'd contained my dress enough to move my legs I propped my foot across my knee to rub it. Usually I walked in flats but I didn't want to risk letting go of Gray before we'd gotten here so I limped back in those killer heels.

Dorian reached out and plucked my ankle off the top of knee and stretched it to his. When he started rubbing the stocking-covered balls of my feet I thought I could orgasm then and there.

"That is amazing. Where did you learn to do that?"

He smiled, a good smile, not a mask but not the showstopper either. "I told you I have experience with uncomfortable shoes. When I was a young man and a woman went off on her own. I'd help her, offer to rub her feet…one thing usually led to another."

"Women used to sleep with you for a foot massage. Wow. You must be good."

He glided his thumb down the tendon on the bottom of my foot and my entire leg shook in response. Well damn.

"Watch it, Gray. We have to keep things civil until we figure it out."

"What are we figuring out?"

To be honest I had no idea. He and I never really talked about what we were or what we could be, only what we couldn't be. I knew I cared about him. I wanted to see where things with him could go. Even after warnings from both Gray and my brother. I wanted to make the choice for my own life. Both of them trying to push me away only made me want what I couldn't have even more.

I decided to go for the truth. "I have absolutely no clue what we need to figure out. But I do know there is something here."

He glanced over as he massaged the entire top portion of my foot in his two big hands. "I agree with that sentiment. We certainly do have something."

I lifted my foot off his lap and he held his hands up for me to switch out the massaged foot for the still aching one.

A moment of silence passed between us while he rubbed, and then he stopped and met my eyes. "If you know what your brother did, then you also know why he felt the need to do it. I agree with him. I'm going mad. And as much as I adore you, Isobel, I refuse to put you in any danger."

His declaration, while well intentioned, punched me in the neck. "And you and my brother are both under the impression that I am unable to take care of myself. I'm a grown woman and if I want to be with a man, insane or not, I'll do what I damn well choose."

My outburst took him by surprise. His eyes flew open wide and the hands that had resumed their ministrations froze.

"Sorry," I grumbled. "I don't like being bossed around, especially by men."

He nodded and started on my feet again. "Understandable. I apologize for presuming to know what is best for you. But I will say, I couldn't live with myself if I hurt you."

I sat up and put my hand over one of his. "You're too late. You leaving, despite it not being of your own free will, that hurt. And you did write that letter. All of that hurt. Then the silence while you brooded. That hurt as well."

He hung his head, a strand of his wavy hair falling forward down his forehead. "I'm sorry for that. I truly am."

I lay back down, if only to get some space between us. "What hurts me most of all is I can't figure out why I care so much. By all accounts we haven't spent a ton of time together. But, whenever I'm with you, it feels like home. Like the home I had before my parents left us. I feel more than happy, more like content. I'm not ready to give that up. Even if that means I have divide my time between my house and the mental institution. Although I have no idea if France has mental institutions."

He chuckled for that one at least. "They do. Plus, money can pretty much buy anything to be delivered anywhere."

I threw my hands up. "There you go. You're rich. Get one of those live-in doctors, except make him a psychologist or whatever. I can't ever remember which ones can prescribe medication. Get one of those. I need a refill on my Xanax."

Another laugh.

When he remained silent I kept going. "Okay then, realistically what are your options? What should you do in this situation?"

He cupped my heel and wiggled it in a way that shot sensation up to my kneecaps. "I should go to the science center where they will likely keep me for observation indefinitely."

"That sounds ominous. Nothing like an American science lab taking prisoners to ruin a relationship."

He continued the silence until it started to piss me off. I dragged my feet of his lap, sat up, and maneuvered the dress until I straddled his lap. He pressed back into the couch as if he were trying to put as much distance between us as possible.

"You're not getting off that easy, Gray. I know you have opinions about this, and feelings. Can you weigh in here? I'm trying to make an effort, and I think you're trying to push me away. Again."

He looked everywhere except at me. Instead of forcing it, I climbed off his lap, went into my bedroom, and slammed the door. I had to get rid of this damn dress. Once I got the zipper off the rest was simple enough. Standing in my underwear, which I'd chosen particularly to inspire worship, his refusal to budge hurt even more.

That man should have been on his knees with his face between my legs right now, and instead, he sat pouting. The consideration of it just didn't feel right. I arranged my boobs in the black corset I wore, made sure the stockings were in place around my thighs, and threw open the door of my bedroom with the same determination with which I slammed it.

"Dorian Gray."

His eyes snapped to mine in the doorway. Then he slowly let his gaze drop down my body in a line. Once he reached my feet he met my eyes again and then glanced off somewhere beside my ear.

"I did not put this corset on for my own benefit."

He flexed his fingers into fists and adjusted on the couch.

When he didn't move, I stalked over in my stocking-clad feet until I stood next to his legs. "Look at me," I snapped.

His eyes flashed to mine.

"It's my turn to take control. And you're going to listen."

DORIAN

This entire plan, to have one last goodbye, had turned into a terrible idea. Sitting on Izzy's couch while she gave me orders in lingerie was not something I was equipped to deal with. Nor was any man if they'd seen the way that lace cupped her breasts.

I swallowed and tried to come up with an excuse to get me out the door. But the second she stepped into her living room in that corset, every problem-solving cell in my body evaporated.

"Nope. Not going to work, Gray."

She reached out and seized one side of my jacket and dragged me to her bedroom. Once inside, she slammed the door, spun me to face her, and then pushed me onto the edge of her bed with two hands against my stomach.

I looked her room over. Her bed was a lovely cherry wood; tones of pale lavender and teal decorated the bedding, furniture, and rug.

"You're not redecorating here. Focus." She ordered. I snapped my attention back and got a face full of her breasts as she unwound my bowtie. The sweet scent of vanilla and peaches rose up from that swell. I could happily spend the rest of eternity with my face in her cleavage.

I met her eyes and the sense of helpless wonder descended once more. There wasn't a single directive she could give that I might deny her.

Instead of trying to fight it, I gave in. She sensed the change immediately, and her movements took on a new level of urgency. As she tried to get my jacket off I stilled her hands and winked. "I got it."

She nodded and knelt to pull my shoes off, then my socks. I'd gotten down to my trousers, undershirt, and cummerbund. All of which she easily stripped too. Now I stood in my pants, intent on playing a more active role in this scenario, but she shook her head and pushed me back down.

The bed bounced and creaked under my weight. When she spun around I caught her intention. The stays of the corset needed to be loosened, and she wanted me to do the honors. I untied the easy knots and loosened the cord until she could wiggle free from the undergarment.

Now clad only in black lace panties and black thigh-high stockings, she made my mouth water. She propped her foot up on my knee and I shuddered, my erection already growing, as I ran a finger under the edge of the sheer fabric and drew it toward me and off her foot.

I reached for her other leg but she slowly lifted the finished one down and spread her balance to lift the other up. In those few seconds, her legs were open, affording me a view of everything she offered.

The second stocking came off faster. Once I'd finished she climbed up onto the bed beside me and leaned in. I matched her, about to press my lips to hers when she put her fingers there instead. It didn't stop me; I drew the middle one between my lips, sucking the end. She rewarded me with a sharp intake of breath and a bite of her lip.

"What do you want me to do?" I asked, hoping and praying it involved me being inside her in the next two minutes.

Her pink lips curled until I feared for any reasonable amount of sanity I had left.

She pushed me to my back and straddled my lap, the heat of her through her panties seeping into my own underwear. That delicious scent of her arousal reached me too, and I cupped her ass to drag her along my erection.

Her eyes fluttered closed and then she jerked and slapped my hands. "I'm in control this time."

I couldn't help but laugh at how seriously she scolded me. With my hands up in surrender I gave her my best innocent bystander look. "I'm at your mercy, My Lady."

She wiggled her hips and I reached out to clutch her hips again. Another swap of my hands. "You do that again, I'm going to punish you."

I released her and allowed her to draw my hands up and anchor them by the wrists with her own near my head. Her lips only centimeters from mine, I tried to close the distance but she pulled back. Once I settled she'd lean in again. Then she kissed me. Not like any kiss she'd shared with me yet. It was purposeful, soft and teasing, and she ran her tongue along the seam of my lips until I relented to her, allowing her inside. Then she let go of my wrists, speared her fingers in the hair behind my ears, and pressed into me harder with her hands, her hips, and that tongue dipping into my mouth, stroking along mine.

Hellfire, I could come in my pants like a teenager from a kiss like this. When she released me and I could form half a coherent thought, I again met her lust-clouded eyes. A satisfied twist of her lips told me she wasn't finished with me yet.

She trailed her lips down my chin, then to the hollow at my throat. Next, a pass over each nipple with a tiny bite that made me reach for her. Then she slid her tongue down the center of my stomach until she reached the edge of my boxer briefs. My cock was so hard the head poked out over the waistband of my pants.

"What have we here?" she asked, before sliding down my legs and jerking my underwear with her. She ripped them off my legs over my feet and dropped them onto the floor. My cock, now free from its confines, sat hard and heavy and waiting for her.

She reached out and grasped it at the base. I could feel that grip all the way to my toes.

"I'm not going to lie. I missed this while you were away doing crazy man things."

I couldn't help but chuckle at the absurdity of her comment. Then she slid her hand up and the laughter gave way to a moan.

"Does that feel good?" she asked, and I could only swallow and nod.

Torn between closing my eyes and giving in to the sensations, and watching as she teased me, I shifted my hips so I could sit up.

"Nope," she said, moving to push me back down but I didn't go.

She raised an eyebrow. It was more of a challenge than a question.

"How about a little game?"

She leaned in, passing her lips against mine for a microsecond before retreating. A tease and a torment. "What kind of game?" Her breath fanned onto my wet lips.

"Do you know *soixante-neuf*?" I asked, before I reached out and cupped the back of her head so when I kissed her this time she couldn't get away. She allowed it, and sucked my bottom lip into her mouth before stalling me again.

"I think you mean sixty-nine, but it does have a certain ring to it in French. It sounds even dirtier if that's possible. What's the game?"

"First one to orgasm loses."

"And the hold out with the amazing focus?" She joked. "What does she win?"

I leaned in and bit her earlobe hard enough to make her suck in a gust of air. "Let's say winner's choice. They can have one wish granted."

She narrowed her eyes. "I'm still not doing anal."

I laughed, kissed her hard, and then lay back on the bed. She scooted back, pulled off her underwear, and shifted into position with her legs spread above my face. I drew her hips down, pressing her thighs wider apart, until I could press my face to her opening.

She smelled like heaven. I licked a line up the wet center of her and her hips shuddered in my hold. This was prize enough for me.

I flicked my tongue over her clit and loosed my hold on one of her thighs to part her lips for a deeper taste.

At the same time, she dropped her mouth down almost to my ball sack and my thoughts fragmented. It took a moment to recall what I was doing until she undulated above me, pressing her pussy into my mouth. I slid my finger along her seam to spread her wide and then I pressed my mouth over her clit and sucked in the little bud. Once I had it in my mouth I re-secured her hips with my hands and teased her mercilessly. She swiveled, gyrated, and humped my face trying to get more pressure there. In turn, she began sucking faster, sliding her hand to my balls downward, slick and hot, each time her mouth came back up, doubling the sensation.

If this woman killed me. I'd go one happy man.

Three minutes of pleasurable torture passed and until she yanked her hips hard away from my arms and climbed off me.

"It doesn't count if you forfeit," I noted, still lying flat.

She shook he head, threw her leg over mine, stood my erection up and sat on it in one long thrust. "You win," she whispered heavily.

I reached out and secured her hips on either side, feeling each silken crook of her hips forward and back. Her eyelids fluttered closed and her neck arched back. Every so often she'd utter a curse or drag her lip between her teeth. I watched it all, trying to focus on her and not the wet hot wrap of her body around my cock.

If I focused on that I'd finish in seconds. And I wanted to make sure she came first.

She canted her hips forward and I could tell this was the position she'd been looking for. Each rise and fall grew more frantic, more frenzied, and she placed her hands on my chest to get better leverage. I let her set the pace and rhythm, merely using her hips to hold onto her, touch her, revel in her.

With no warning I felt the first squeeze of her orgasm, and it triggered mine like a semi truck striking another head on. I clutched her hips harder and let her ride out the end of her own orgasm. Once she started to slow I took hold and fucked myself with her body. It was wetter and tighter from her own end, and mine burst forth. I came fast and hard lifting my hips up bringing us a little off the bed now. She held on until I stilled and then lay down flat on my chest with me still clutched tight in the hold of her body.

Damn. I wrapped my hand around her neck, sliding my fingers through her silken hair.

"That felt good," she whispered against my sweat-sheened chest.

I could only smile. She mumbled something about a good one

before her eyes fluttered shut and she burrowed her face into the dip of my chest.

How I had ever considered giving this woman up I couldn't understand. It was as if the moment I left the warm embrace of her body I forgot how perfect she feels in my arms. Every single inch of her inspired adoration. I was a fool to think I could leave her for some other man to claim.

I'd rather die than witness that tragedy.

She mumbled again and I ran my hands over the top of her head, smoothing and petting her hair in gentle strokes. When she stilled, I grabbed a blanket we'd shuffled over in our haste and spread it on top of us.

A soft knock at her apartment door dragged me from the edge of sleep. When it didn't repeat, I forgot all about it and succumbed to slumber, still inside the woman of my dreams.

IZZY

I woke to the scent of bacon. Definitely not a bad thing, but a strange one for my apartment. My cooking skills weren't legendary. I slipped on a T-shirt and a pair of boyshorts before investigating.

Dorian stood at my counter, eating a slice of bacon shirtless, in his dress pants, reading the local newspaper. More food covered the countertop and the longer I stared at him the weirder the scene became. He appeared relaxed, and not in a way I'd seen him yet. A strange mix of content and leisure.

"You saved me some, right?" I asked to alert him to my presence.

He glanced up and gave me a smile. The one I really liked. The one I was beginning to think he reserved only for me. "Good morning, how are you feeling?"

I scoped out the spread and sat down on the stool in front of an empty plate. "You mean, if my brother hadn't kidnapped you, this is what I had to look forward to the other night?"

Instead of answering me he came around the bar, slid his hands around my waist, and drew me in for a kiss. Coffee and bacon were on his lips, and I didn't mind in the least. It was a quick kiss, one meant for good mornings before soft sweet lovemaking. But he didn't take me back to bed, he did the next best thing and handed over a mug of fresh coffee.

He released me and went back to standing in front of the newspaper. I leaned over to scope it out, but of course, the paper had been printed in French. "How many languages do you speak?"

He turned the page. "About ten. Most of the romantics and a little Arabic and Farsi."

A man of many talents. I took a sip of my coffee and propped my feet up to draw my knees into my arms. "Oh just a little Arabic and Farsi, huh?"

I watched him for a while before idly spinning on the stool between sips. A brown box sitting by the door caught my attention. "What is that?" I asked as I pointed to it.

He glanced up and scratched his cheek. His five o'clock shadow was already making him look a little rugged and sexy. "I don't know. I think it was delivered last night. I grabbed it this morning before I went to the market. It was just sitting against your doorframe."

I placed the mug on the counter, grabbed the box, and returned to my stool. There was an envelope taped to the top of the brown Kraft tape securing it closed. The envelope pulled off easily, so I ripped it open and unfolded the plain white paper inside. My brother's handwriting immediately caused me to clutch the paper tighter.

Dear P,

There was more I didn't tell you about that night. I spoke to his scientists and they have a possible cure in the works, but for now they have a daily injection for their patients that works as sort of a hard drive backup, fortifying the brain's synapses.

I didn't want to tell you, hoping that if you two stayed apart then it wouldn't matter anyway. Also, I don't want you to murder me when we go on vacation to Italy.

Be safe. I love you.

J

I pointed toward the drawer urgently and Dorian got the hint. In two seconds I had a knife in my hand and the box open on my counter. Inside sat rows of bottles and a package of syringes.

"What is it?" he asked.

Answering him would take too long. I handed him Jake's note and pulled a small glass vial from the box. It didn't have the usual prescription number on it, instead the vial read 52.

Dorian dropped the paper to the counter and reached in to pull out an identical bottle. "He's telling the truth."

"How do you know?" I asked, still studying the clear liquid.

"That's the number on all my case files. I was the 52nd person they studied."

The revelation sank in. "How many of you are there?"

He shook his head still inspecting the bottle. "I have no idea."

Now I was curious. "I wonder how old the oldest study they have is—it's fascinating." I was avoiding asking the obvious questions. The hard ones that I knew could take him away from me.

The silence stretched as he pulled out each individual vial and then read a small card in the bottom of the box. "How did your brother even get access to this?"

I shrugged. "He can pretty much get access to anything if you ask him nicely."

"Your brother is a dangerous man," he said, finally placing the last bottle in line with the other ten.

I didn't bother responding to that since he knew first-hand how Jake could be. "Are you going to take it?" I finally asked. One of us needed to.

He leaned down so his eyes were level with the medication. "I'm not entirely sure. I'd like to discuss it with the doctor first, just in case. What if there are side effects Jake didn't mention or know about?"

Neither of us voiced the other question. *What if your brother is just trying to kill me?*

"And in the meantime, while you figure this out?"

He glanced up at me over the vials. "In the meantime I think I should stay away from you."

Even knowing what he was going to say, it still hurt. Like a sledgehammer to the sternum. I wished I were the kind of woman who threw a fit about what she wanted. The kind who would use any and all means to make him stay. But that wasn't me. I refused to convince a man to stay with me, even if I wanted him to.

Instead I grabbed my cup and a slice of bacon, and slid off the stool. When I reached my bedroom door I turned back. "You do what you have to do."

I entered and threw myself on the chair by the window so I could think about the situation. Thinking Gray would take his things and leave, I didn't expect him to enter the room a few minutes later. "Are you okay?"

I didn't want to look at him right now, especially with the scent of him clinging to every inch of my skin. "I'm fine."

He sat on the bed facing me. "I've been around a few years. I know the look and tone of a woman who is definitely not fine."

Finally, I met his eyes. "I'm not going to ask you to stay with me. I want you to, and I think we would have a lot of fun together. But you've made up your mind about how you want to proceed. I'm not going to be able to change it, so why should I try?"

He blinked. Maybe he didn't expect me to be so honest. Most men I'd spent time with in my life didn't.

"And what would you have me do? Endanger you?"

"How is a week from now, a month from now, any different than what we did last night? And what we were just doing in my kitchen, or over the last week? Is it different now because you know your mind is deteriorating, or is it different because I'm not Sibyl?"

I blinked rapidly and took in a big breath of air. I hadn't expected quite that much truth to come out.

"Is that your fear? That I'm pushing you away since you play no factor in my journey to rectify my sins? You think I don't care about you now that I know you're not her?"

I didn't answer, and instead stared out the window. If I looked at him, I knew I'd climb out of the chair and go to him.

"You should know; I knew you were nothing like her from the first day you told me off in the square." He dropped to his knees in the carpet and shuffled forward until he could put his hands on my legs. "She was meek and you're strong. She was giving only to receive, whereas you give because it's the only way you know how to be. She was a child and you are a woman. Even if my mind couldn't visibly see the differences, I know very well you are not her. And she could never live up to you. Not the other way around."

Damn. What did I say to that? I met his eyes, and there was a sincerity there that reached inside my chest and broke down every single wall I'd ever created to keep people out. The bastard kept doing that. Tearing into my heart and my memories and the way I saw the world.

"I only want to protect you," he said, before laying his face, cheek down, on my curled up calves.

I ran my fingers through his silky soft hair. "I don't know what's going to happen, but I'll wait and see because I want to be with you."

He lifted his head and I shifted my hand to the side of his face. "Why would you do that? You don't know how long it might take for me to become stable."

"Because I want you. And if this is the only way I can have you, so be it."

"I think I could fall in love with you, Isobel Vale."

I sat my coffee mug on wide window sill and leaned down to press my lips to his gently. Then pulled back enough to meet his eyes. "I know you could. Why wouldn't you?"

He growled, an actual growl, before sliding his arms under me, lifting me up, and throwing me on my bed. Before I could right myself, he crawled between my open thighs. "I want to hear you say it," he said.

A laugh bubbled out before I could reel it back. "Say what?"

He lifted my shirt and bit the side of my waist hard enough that I swore and swatted at his shoulders. Once he released me he met my eyes again. "Say it."

I feigned innocence but wiggled my hips into him, his erection already greeting my movements. "Say what?" I asked, this time a little more breathlessly.

He shifted up my body until we aligned in that oh-so-beautiful way. "Say it," he whispered.

"I think I could fall in love with you too, Dorian Gray."

He smiled and the corners of his eyes crinkled up, and looking at him was like trying to look into the face of the sun. I wanted to earn that smile every single damn day. "I'll take that," he said.

With a sigh he surged his hips up against me and I stalled his shoulders. "Nope, Mister. This is not keeping your distance."

He kissed the curve of my neck and I tried to hold on to whatever argument I formed in my mind. But it was fleeing fast under his mouth

Somehow the man had already discerned that I loved the way it felt when he nibbled on my earlobe, and as he drew one between his lips and sucked on it gently I began unbuckling his belt.

"Let's just start that distance-keeping thing on Monday," I whispered before using my feet to push his pants down his legs.

It was hours before either of us spoke again.

EPILOGUE
DORIAN
SIX MONTHS LATER

"Just stick it in. I promise I'll be fine." I told her.

She didn't look convinced as she crouched, her eyes on the swell of my ass. "Are you sure you want me to do this? Obviously you have more practice at it."

"You offered to assist."

She let out a long sigh and then stuck the needle in the fleshy part of my behind. I flinched slightly at the sharp sting and the cold that spread as she pressed the plunger.

"Ok, done."

She wiped the area with an alcohol swab and I pulled up my

pants and refastened my belt buckle.

The needle went into a biohazard bucket and I placed the vial back in the refrigerator. She parked herself on my countertop, where she usually sat as I cooked these days. "We need to talk."

I started pulling vegetables from the lower drawers and sat them beside her on the counter. "Oh?"

"That ring you gave me is not going to work for me."

I snorted, grabbed the last eggplant, and closed the refrigerator door. "You mean the two-carat-formerly-owned-by-a-princess engagement ring I gave you? Or some other ring?"

She rolled her eyes and shifted, waiting for me to be serious.

"Fine, what's wrong with it?" I asked.

"Besides the fact that I'd need a security detail to wear it out of the house, I can't put my hands in my jeans pocket. It gets caught on the edge. If you want me to marry you then you'll need to give me a smaller diamond."

I froze in the act of grabbing a knife from the drawer and went back to stand in front of her. "Are you complaining about the engagement ring I got you?"

She bit her bottom lip. "Not complaining, but more like registering a concern. It's gorgeous and I love it, but I'm terrified I'm going to lose it and the deposit on the insurance claim is probably more than my apartment in New York."

I gripped her waist and pulled her in. When she wrapped her legs around my hips and her arms around my neck, I knew dinner was going to have to wait. "I'm going to tell you this again, because I think you might not be understanding me. When we get married, you will be rich. All of my considerable fortune will be yours."

"How considerable are we talking here?" she whispered, leaning in to brush her lips against mine.

I pressed my swelling erection into her core. "Enormous. Gratuitously so."

The laugh that filtered through her vibrated into my chest where we touched. "Fine, I'll stop complaining."

Finally, I'd gotten the woman to compromise. "I should finish this food."

She shook her head and started on the buttons nearest my throat. "I know exactly what we should do."

I carried her to my bed and tossed her on top of the duvet. When she had moved in, she'd switched my color palette to shades of maroon and black. It suited the rest of the décor and I loved the idea of her making my home her own.

"Soon you'll be Mrs. Gray."

She made a face at me.

"What, are you going to object to my name too?"

"I think I should keep my own name," she said.

I climbed up beside her and lay down so she could face me. "You're going to have to explain your reasoning."

"I don't want people to start equating me to that book."

"I think outside of high school literature classes, you're pretty safe."

She swatted at my chest and shifted closer to entwine our legs. "No, not that damn book."

It took me entirely too long to figure out what she was saying. "To be fair, imagine if you'd had to deal with it through the entire process of publication and then movie rights."

"I'm glad I didn't have to and I want to avoid it in the future."

I leaned down and nibbled on her neck and collarbone before speaking again. "You mean you don't want Fifty Shades of Gray?"

She sighed aloud and I closed my eyes, committing the sound to memory. Those little noises she made could get me hard in seconds.

"No, I don't need Fifty Shades when I have the original. Just one shade of Gray suits me fine."

ACKNOWLEDGMENTS

There are so many people I need to thank for helping me with this book. The NCOWs, the Blackship Fangirls, for a start. My lovely beta readers: Cherly Demont and Karlee Lawrence. Nancy Smay, my excellent editor.

As I mentioned in the dedication, Margie Lawson. If you know you then you know why, if you don't then you need to meet her.

Uh…Todd Skaggs for reading and encouraging me through Dorian's entire book. Uncle Dudley's Restaurant for fueling me with those crack hash browns.

If I missed you in this acknowledgement, I apologize. Call it author exhaustion and I'll get you on the next round.

ABOUT THE AUTHOR

Monica Corwin is a *New York Times* and *USA Today* bestselling author. She is an outspoken writer attempting to make romance accessible to everyone, no matter their preferences. As a Northern Ohioian, Monica enjoys snow drifts, three seasons of weather, and a dislike of Michigan football. Monica owns more books about King Arthur than should be strictly necessary. Also typewriters...lots and lots of typewriters.

YOU CAN JOIN HER NEWSLETTER LIST BY GOING HERE:
HTTP://MADMIMI.COM/SIGNUPS/267423/JOIN